This month, in
LONE STAR KNIGHT
by Cindy Gerard,
meet Matthew Walker—owner of
a ranching empire. The only thing missing from
Matt's life was the love of a good woman, until...
he crossed paths with the Lady Helena Reichard,
whose heart he was determined to win!

**SILHOUETTE DESIRE
IS PROUD TO PRESENT THE**

Five wealthy Texas bachelors—all members of
the state's most exclusive club—set out to restore
the "Royal" jewels...and find true love.

* * *

And don't miss
HER ARDENT SHEIKH
by Kristi Gold,
next month's installment of the
Texas Cattleman's Club: Lone Star Jewels,
available only in Silhouette Desire!

Dear Reader,

Welcome to the world of Silhouette Desire, where you can indulge yourself every month with romances that can only be described as passionate, powerful and provocative!

The incomparable Diana Palmer heads the Desire lineup for March. *The Winter Soldier* is a continuation of the author's popular cross-line miniseries, SOLDIERS OF FORTUNE. We're sure you'll enjoy this tale of a jaded hero who offers protection in the form of a marriage of convenience to a beautiful woman in jeopardy.

Bestselling author Leanne Banks offers you March's MAN OF THE MONTH, a tempting *Millionaire Husband,* book two of her seductive miniseries MILLION DOLLAR MEN. The exciting Desire continuity series TEXAS CATTLEMAN'S CLUB: LONE STAR JEWELS continues with *Lone Star Knight* by Cindy Gerard, in which a lady of royal lineage finds love with a rugged Texas cattle baron.

The M.D. Courts His Nurse as Meagan McKinney's miniseries MATCHED IN MONTANA returns to Desire. And a single-dad rancher falls for the sexy horsetrainer he unexpectly hires in Kathie DeNosky's *The Rough and Ready Rancher*. To cap off the month, Shawna Delacorte writes a torrid tale of being *Stormbound with a Tycoon*.

So make some special time for yourself this month, and read all six of these tantalizing Silhouette Desires!

Enjoy!

Joan Marlow Golan

Joan Marlow Golan
Senior Editor, Silhouette Desire

Please address questions and book requests to:
Silhouette Reader Service
U.S.: 3010 Walden Ave., P.O. Box 1325, Buffalo, NY 14269
Canadian: P.O. Box 609, Fort Erie, Ont. L2A 5X3

Lone Star Knight

CINDY GERARD

Silhouette® Desire®

Published by Silhouette Books

America's Publisher of Contemporary Romance

If you purchased this book without a cover you should be aware
that this book is stolen property. It was reported as "unsold and
destroyed" to the publisher, and neither the author nor the
publisher has received any payment for this "stripped book."

Special thanks and acknowledgment are given to Cindy Gerard for her
contribution to the Texas Cattleman's Club: Lone Star Jewels series.

New friends, like blessings, turn up at the most unexpected times.
This book is dedicated to my new friends, talented authors all:
Jennifer Greene, Sara Orwig, Kristi Gold and Sheri WhiteFeather.
It was great fun saving the jewels with you.

Special thanks to Dr. Joan Harding for lending both her friendship
and her medical expertise to the writing of this book.

 SILHOUETTE BOOKS

ISBN 0-373-76353-0

LONE STAR KNIGHT

Copyright © 2001 by Harlequin Books S.A.

All rights reserved. Except for use in any review, the reproduction
or utilization of this work in whole or in part in any form by any
electronic, mechanical or other means, now known or hereafter
invented, including xerography, photocopying and recording, or in
any information storage or retrieval system, is forbidden without
the written permission of the editorial office, Silhouette Books,
300 East 42nd Street, New York, NY 10017 U.S.A.

All characters in this book have no existence outside the imagination of
the author and have no relation whatsoever to anyone bearing the same
name or names. They are not even distantly inspired by any individual
known or unknown to the author, and all incidents are pure invention.

This edition published by arrangement with Harlequin Books S.A.

® and TM are trademarks of Harlequin Books S.A., used under license.
Trademarks indicated with ® are registered in the United States Patent
and Trademark Office, the Canadian Trade Marks Office and in other
countries.

Visit Silhouette at www.eHarlequin.com

Printed in U.S.A.

Books by Cindy Gerard

Silhouette Desire

The Cowboy Takes a Lady #957
Lucas: The Loner #975
*The Bride Wore Blue #1012
*A Bride for Abel Greene #1052
*A Bride for Crimson Falls #1076
†The Outlaw's Wife #1175
†Marriage, Outlaw Style #1185
†The Outlaw Jesse James #1198
Lone Star Prince #1256
In His Loving Arms #1293
Lone Star Knight #1353

*Northern Lights Brides
†Outlaw Hearts

CINDY GERARD

If asked "What's your idea of heaven?" Cindy Gerard would say a warm sun, a cool breeze, pan pizza and a good book. If she had to settle for one of the four, she'd opt for the book, with the pizza running a close second. Inspired by the pleasure she's received from the books she's read and her longtime love affair with her husband, Tom, Cindy now creates her own evocative and sensual love stories about compelling characters and complex relationships.

This number-one bestselling author of close to twenty books has received numerous industry awards, among them the National Readers' Choice Award, multiple *Romantic Times Magazine* nominations and two RITA Award nominations from the Romance Writers of America.

"What's Happening in Royal?"

NEWS FLASH, March—There are reports that the glamorous Lady Helena Reichard is hiding in Royal, TX. After sustaining injuries from the emergency crash landing of her plane two months ago, she was reportedly released from the hospital—and then vanished! Countless paparazzi stationed outside the medical building have been left disappointed…where can Lady Helena be?

Some are speculating that tycoon rancher Matthew Walker could be protecting her from the glaring cameras and photographers' flashes by nestling her away on the palatial grounds of his High Stakes Ranch. This Texas Cattleman's Club member is known for his honor when it comes to the ladies…but Lady Helena's blond, tantalizing beauty *is* world-renowned!

Could her disappearance be linked to the two suspicious-looking men seen lurking about town? Perhaps our boys at the Cattleman's Club would fill us in? Stay tuned.…

Prologue

It wasn't true. Not completely. Your entire life didn't flash
before you when you were about to die. Only bits and
pieces, odd, unrelated little snippets scrolled by like a vivid
Technicolor collage—along with an extreme and acute
awareness of those who were about to die with you.

While the flight crew and eleven other men and women
in the charter jet bound from Royal, Texas, to the European country of Asterland prepared for the crash with stal-
wart optimism, whispered prayers, or soft weeping, Lady
Helena Reichard thought silently of Asterland, the home
she might never see again. She thought of her parents, the
Earl and Countess of Orion, and the pain her death would
cause them. Of the calico kitten she'd loved as a child, the
projects she might not be around to finish and of those
who might suffer because of that.

Oddly, she also thought of the tall, handsome Texan
with smiling green eyes and dark curling hair who had

waltzed her around the dance floor at the Texas Cattle-man's Club reception just two nights past.

She'd met commanding men before. Sophisticated. Worldly. Titled and moneyed. She hadn't, however, met anyone like Matthew Walker. With his quick, slashing smile and devastating wit, he'd been at once charming yet subtly and purposefully aloof. He was obviously a man of wealth, yet the hand that had held hers in its strong grip had worn the calluses of physical labor without apology. His polished and gallant formality had been a fascinating foil for an understated man-of-the-earth essence that had both intrigued and captivated—and left her wishing she hadn't had to leave Royal, Texas, so soon.

How sad, she thought, that she'd been denied the chance to know him better. How sad that her last glimpse of Texas would be from five hundred feet and falling. And then she thought of nothing but the moment as the jet, its left engine shooting fire, lurched, shuddered and dropped the last one hundred feet to the ground. She lowered her head, wrapped her arms around her ankles and prepared for the impact.

Behind her someone screamed. A serrated, grating screech ripped through the pressurized cabin as tons of steel and flammable fuel slammed to earth then skidded across the desert floor without benefit of landing gear. The noise was shattering. The jolt, bone-rattling. And the fear—the fear was paralyzing as the flames that had been confined to the left jet suddenly engulfed the cabin and a blinding, screaming pain consumed her.

One

"Justin—hey, Justin, wait up." Matt Walker was striding wearily toward the burn-unit nurses' station when he spotted Justin Webb, dressed in green scrubs, heading for the elevator.

Justin turned, sipping from a paper cup that Matt knew held the world's worst coffee. After a long, critical once-over he scowled, showing Matt his doctor's face. "I've done admits on patients who look better than you."

Matt knew exactly what his friend saw: a five-o'clock shadow, badly rumpled shirt and bloodshot eyes. He scrubbed a hand over his unshaven jaw, rolled the stiffness out of his shoulders. "I'm fine. Just a long night."

Justin snorted. "More like a lot of long nights."

When he extended the coffee Matt grimaced and made a warding sign. "How do you drink that sludge?"

"Cast-iron stomach." Justin flashed a grin. "Besides— I like it. But we were talking about you. You knock yourself out from sleep deprivation and you're not going to be any good to her, Matt.''

Both men knew exactly who Justin was talking about. It had been almost two months since the plane crash that had resulted in Lady Helena Reichard's emergency admission to the burn unit at Royal Memorial Hospital. She had been among a group of Asterland dignitaries and a few locals—Matt's friends Pamela Black and Jamie Morris among them—who were en route to Asterland after a posh diplomatic reception at the Texas Cattleman's Club. Close to a full month had passed since Matt had been assigned by his fellow club members to stand guard outside Helena's door.

It didn't much matter that he was beat. His welfare wasn't at stake here. Helena's was. He just wished he knew who, or what, he was protecting her from.

Besides Matt and Justin, only three other club members knew the mysterious details surrounding the charter jet's emergency landing that had sent Helena to the hospital. Though luckily no one had been killed, even now, two months later, it was still tough to absorb. The crash had been bad enough. But there'd also been a murder. A jewel theft. The hint of an attempted political coup involving the European country of Asterland.

Helena Reichard, it seemed, was stuck smack in the middle of it all; Matt understood exactly how vulnerable she was. He also understood that nothing, absolutely nothing more was going to happen to her under his watch.

''How's she doing?'' he asked, as Justin drained the cup then tossed it into a trash bin.

''Well, to hear her tell it, she's doing just fine.''

Matt studied his friend's face. ''I think I'd rather hear you tell it. How is she, really?''

Justin crossed his arms over his chest, gave Matt a considering look. "We've covered this ground before."

"Humor me. Cover it again."

"Look, I'm not the primary here—I'm just consulting until she's ready for the cosmetic repairs. Harding's on the burns. Chambers is her bone man. But the charts pretty much speak for themselves."

"Not to me they don't." Matt shifted his weight to one hip. "Suppose you fill me in."

"You're not family, Matt."

"Oh, for the—"

"Wait. Wait." Justin held up a hand. "Cool down. You're not family *but,* since you're all she's got standing between her and Lord knows what might be a threat to her, you have a need to know. And that gives me license to tell you."

After a glance toward the charge nurse who was busy on the phone, he steered Matt toward the sofa at the end of the hall on the pretense of privacy. Matt suspected what Justin really wanted was to get him off his feet. Too tired to make an issue of it, he sat.

"As you already know, most of her burns are second degree and restricted to her left arm and upper leg." Justin eased down beside him. "It's that nasty patch of third degree on the back of her left hand that's giving her trouble. The extensor tendons are heavily involved—the ones that control finger movement. We had to graft. Unfortunately, the site's been problematic."

Matt slumped back, rubbed an index finger over his brow. "Infection, right?"

Justin nodded. "We'd hoped to avoid it—we always hope to avoid it—but with a burn that deep and so much debris ground into it, it was pretty much a given. It's cleared up now but it set her recovery back. Only time will tell what kind of mobility she'll regain.''

Matt thought of the lovely hand he'd held in his at the Cattleman's Club reception and dance. The petal-soft skin. The slim, graceful fingers. ''And her ankle?''

Justin shook his head. ''That's still up for grabs, too. It's a bad fracture. Real bad. Even with the surgery and the pins in place, Chambers can't guarantee that she won't have a permanent limp.''

Matt stared past Justin's shoulder to the partially open door of Helena's room. He thought of the beautiful, vivacious woman he'd waltzed around the dance floor. The woman whose cornflower-blue eyes had smiled into his with unguarded interest. The woman who had said his name in her perfect, practiced English yet made it sound exotic and made him feel extraordinary. That woman had been beyond perfection.

He didn't have to be inside her head to understand that the woman in the hospital room, though still beautiful, was now badly scarred, potentially disabled—and that there would be much more to her recovery process than knitting bones and healing flesh. And he couldn't throw the helpless notion that there wasn't a damn thing he could do to help her.

''You need sleep, bud.'' Justin's voice broke into Matt's thoughts. ''Call someone to relieve you.''

''Not an option. Not tonight anyway. My men are tied up, so I'm it.''

After a long look, Justin rose. ''Okay. Here's the plan. I've got a patient on the floor spiking a temp so I'll be here for a while. I can cover for you for a few hours.''

''Thanks, but she's *my* assignment, not yours.''

Justin's long, measuring look asked the same question

Matt had been asking himself lately. *Are you sure this is just an assignment?*

Matt wasn't sure of anything except that he wasn't ready to admit, even to himself, that it might be more. Yeah, he recognized that his commitment to her safety was running a tad toward territorial. He also knew that he found himself thinking about her more than he should. Helena was, after all, an intriguing woman. Not his type of woman, but intriguing, nonetheless.

Regardless, it all came down to one thing. The five club members who were in the know on this incident agreed that Lady Helena Reichard was his responsibility. It was a charge he took seriously. Even more so after what had happened last week. He'd ducked out for a moment and come back to find a strange man standing just outside her open doorway. The man had run like hell when Matt had approached him, and in the darkened hall, he'd never even got a glimpse of his face. Whoever it was, he was still out there. Judging by his actions, he was also a potential threat.

"I'm not going anywhere, Justin," he stated flatly.

"Yeah," Justin said with quiet authority. "You are."

He pointed to the room across the hall from Helena's. "The bed in there is empty. Use it. I'm taking your watch for a few hours. End of story."

When Matt opened his mouth to protest, Justin cut him off. "Use it," he ordered and walked to the nurses' station to grab some charts.

Helena stared out her hospital-room window into the predawn darkness of the West Texas morning. The nightmare had awakened her. Again. As she so often did, she sat in the dark and fought a losing battle with haunting memories of the crash.

She swallowed back the slick ball of nausea that rose to

her throat. Almost two months of endless nights had passed, and she still hadn't been able to come to terms with what had happened to her. And with what hadn't.

She hadn't died. Miraculously, no one had. In fact, she and Robert Klimt, a member of King Bertram's cabinet, were the only ones who had been seriously injured. Yes, she had lived, but her injuries were a constant, vengeful reminder that life, as she'd known it, would never be the same again.

A helpless anger flushed her skin as she carefully peeled the protective pressure glove—her constant companion for at least the next year—from her left hand. She made herself look at it. At the disfiguring patch of grafted flesh, the repulsive scarring, the stiff, useless fingers that might never again hold a champagne glass, might never wear a ring or be lifted to a man's lips for a lingering kiss.

She pushed back her sleeve and forced her gaze to travel the angry red scars that ran almost to her elbow. Touching her hand to the insulted flesh, she shivered at the dry, hot feel of it then grimly flipped back the long folds of the hospital gown that covered her legs.

More painful even than her broken ankle and the six-inch surgical incisions running on either side of it beneath the cast, more painful even than the burns, was the donor site on her leg. A four-by-three-inch patch of skin had been harvested from her outer thigh to graft to the back of her hand. It still looked raw. It still gave her pain. The hope was that it would also give her back the use of her hand.

That was the hope.

She covered her leg, tucked her hand into the folds of her robe, and hated herself for giving in to self-pity. Robert Klimt still fought for his life. She did not know him well. She knew only that he lay in a coma and might not recover. Yet she sat here feeling sorry for herself because her perfection had been marred.

"Beauty such as yours is a rare gift, child. You are a jewel. A precious, flawless gem to be adored and revered by the world as a priceless treasure."

Her father's words, words she'd heard and believed since she'd been old enough to crawl up on his knee and bask in his adoration, echoed relentlessly through her mind.

"Not anymore, Papa." She stared into the hollow, echoing silence. "I'm not flawless anymore."

Matthew Walker had thought she was perfect. She had seen it in his eyes, eyes she'd envisioned too often in her mind since the crash. She'd heard it in his laughter, laughter that brightened her dreams, but never her days. She'd thought he would come to the hospital to see her. For conflicting reasons, she'd been both disappointed and relieved when he hadn't.

She stared again at the hand that no longer seemed to belong to her, at the mass of ugly scars, the stiffened fingers that refused to work as they once had.

Matthew Walker would not think that she was perfect now.

No one would.

She raised her head, stared without seeing, as the blackness of night slowly gave way to the pearly gray break of another dawn. Artificial light from the hall behind her shone in through her door, casting the room in half shadows. A call bell pinged softly at the nurses' desk; a doctor's page echoed in this sterile, isolated world where the silence spoke of an aloneness only someone who had spent myriad sleepless nights swathed in bandages and morphine and uncertainty could understand.

She had become accustomed to the night sounds in the

burn unit for she had slept too little and thought too much. Now, in the background, the nursing staff moved with quiet efficiency to the soft rustle of crepe-soled shoes and pristine white uniforms.

She hadn't rung for their assistance when she'd inched carefully out of bed and eased into the chair by the window. She'd been managing that particular feat by herself for over a week now. The fine sheen of perspiration beading her brow was the only outward indication of the physical cost. The tear that trickled unheeded down her cheek was less a result of the pain than of the growing and grim acceptance that she would never be, would never look, the same again—and that the waltz she had shared with the tall, handsome Texan might have been her last dance.

Matt scrubbed a hand over his face as he stood like a shadow in the doorway of Helena's room. He didn't know if he felt better or worse for the three hours of sleep Justin had insisted he grab. He figured he had to feel better than she did.

He didn't much like fighting this constant urge to go to her. Just talk to her. Maybe make her smile as she'd smiled for him one night that now seemed a lifetime ago.

Her smiles aren't your concern, though, are they? he reminded himself grimly. Her protection was.

And yet, she looked so lost as she sat there. So absolutely alone. Nothing like the self-assured, sensual woman who'd shamelessly and skillfully flirted with him on the dance floor at the club. It tore him up, that look, and yet he didn't want her to know he was there—watching that silken length of pale blond hair fall across her face as she hung her head and battled the tears welling up in her eyes. He didn't want her to know he was remembering the texture and the scent of her hair trailing across his fingers as they'd danced around the room while he'd smiled into her laughing eyes.

Pride, he'd discovered this past month, was a quality Lady Helena owned in abundance. She wouldn't want to know that anyone had witnessed her struggle—or her pain. Neither would she want to know that he'd been holding vigil outside her room. Or that the reason he was here was to protect her from an unknown enemy, with an as-yet-undetermined agenda. He didn't want her to know it either. She had enough to deal with without adding a possible threat to her life to the list.

He cupped his palm to his nape, stepped silently away from the door and tried to sort it all out in his mind. He wasn't exactly up on his cloak-and-dagger etiquette—it had been a while since he'd been called on to draw from his military background—but he'd come up to speed in a hurry. Anyone wanting to get to Helena was going to have to get through him.

Damn, he didn't like what was happening. Didn't like any of it. The only good news unearthed lately was that the investigation into the plane crash had turned up evidence that it had actually been an accident that had caused the emergency landing, not sabotage as they had originally suspected. An engine fire had caused some of the systems to lock up, including the landing gear. On impact, liquor bottles in the bar had broken, the electrical systems inside the luxury charter jet had shorted out and sparks had ignited the flammable liquor. Helena, sitting closest to the bar, had paid the biggest price.

So yeah, thankfully, they'd ruled out sabotage, but nothing else was resolved. He wished to hell he could get a handle on it.

"Okay, Walker," he muttered and sank down on the

small sofa by the window in the corridor just outside Helena's room, "start at point A."

Point A, the Lone Star jewels—three precious gems entrusted through generations to the Club members' keeping—had been stolen. Before this nasty business, he'd never actually seen the jewels. Like every Cattleman's Club member, he had sworn to protect them as part of Royal's legacy of prosperity. Like every other Royal resident, he'd known of them through folklore and legend and had, from time to time, wondered if they actually existed. Well, he wasn't wondering any longer. He'd seen two of them himself after Justin had recovered them at the crash site. The black opal—representing justice—was magnificent. The emerald—representing peace—was dazzling. He'd held both in his hands and damn if he hadn't felt a dynamic sense of—

Of what? He shook his head, not wanting to believe that even now, almost two months later, he was still convinced that they'd warmed his palm with energy and heat.

He shrugged that off and concentrated on point B—the missing stone, a rare red diamond. The diamond represented leadership and completed the circle of prosperity upon which Royal was dependent. The big question that remained was where the devil was it? And if it wasn't found and reunited with the other stones, would Royal's thriving economy fold like a tower of cards as the legend predicted?

Since he didn't have the answers to any of those questions, he moved ahead to point C. Riley Monroe was dead. Riley had been a fixture behind the bar at the Cattleman's Club even before Matt had been initiated into the ranks. Anger didn't begin to cover what he felt for the scum who had killed him. And all because they'd wanted the jewels.

That indisputable conclusion only brought up more

questions. How had an outsider actually found out about the jewels' existence, discovered their hiding place and then stolen them? Why were the opal and the emerald on that plane bound for Asterland? Again, another dead end, another set of unanswered questions.

Leaning forward, he propped his forearms on his thighs and stared at his loosely clasped hands. Okay. Point D. Milo Yungst and Garth Johannes. Talk about cloak-and-dagger.

When the four other club members who were in the know on this mission had last met, he'd confided to them his concerns about the pair.

"I don't care that Yungst and Johannes are representatives from the Asterland government. I don't give a good damn that they were sent to investigate the plane crash."

He'd looked around the private meeting room at the Cattleman's Club at Justin Webb, Aaron Black, Sheikh Ben Rassad and Dakota Lewis. "I don't trust them. And I don't like their methods. I like even less the interrogation tactics they used on Pamela."

He'd seen from the dark scowl on Aaron's face that he was in agreement. Pamela had been on the plane with Helena and Jamie Morris. Pamela was also Matt's good friend. He'd given her away the day she'd married Aaron. Now that she was his wife, Aaron had more than a vested interest in Pamela's welfare.

And that's what brought Matt to point E and the reason he was here, outside Helena's hospital room. It was at that meeting that they'd decided Jamie and Helena needed protection. Ben had been assigned to guard Jamie. Matt had volunteered to watch over Helena—an assignment the five of them had agreed was necessary until they unraveled the mystery and were sure the women were safe.

At least it had started out as an assignment. Maybe it

was fatigue—maybe not—but he was finally ready to admit that somewhere along the line, it had ended up feeling like more.

Well, he couldn't afford to let it be more. Couldn't let *her* be more. Not to him. And still, it was the *more* that compelled him to rise and walk back to her room. Shoving his hands in his back pockets, he leaned a shoulder against the doorjamb and studied the beautiful, tortured profile that had haunted him for as many nights as he'd known her.

In the diluted light, he looked at her solemn profile. He looked at her damaged hand, at her leg in an immobilizing cast that ran from toe to mid-calf. His mouth set in a grim line, he tried to shake one niggling question. If this was just an assignment, why did he find himself wanting to heal those hurts that her eyes betrayed but that she would never admit to?

Two

Helena knew she was dreaming. She knew it because in the dream she was perfect and she was whole. Still…it felt so immediate, so real and oh, so preferable to the nightmare that always concluded with searing flames and brutal pain.

Oh, yes. She liked this dream so much better.

In it, she was in the middle of a grand ballroom. A gentle mist drifted at her feet as if conjured by a medieval mage from a swirl of stardust and moonbeams. She floated with the fantasy of it, seeing herself as she'd once been. Her left hand was smooth and pale, a perfect, graceful backdrop for the pearl-and-ruby ring that had been her mother's and her grandmother's before her.

Her dress was the same blue as her eyes. It was also strapless and shamelessly seductive. The parchment-thin, watery silk clung to the full curve of her breasts, nipped in at her waist then hugged her hips to end at mid-thigh and reveal the long, unblemished length of her legs, show-case her slender ankles in three-inch heels.

That there were no scars to hide, no broken bones as yet unhealed, wasn't even the best part. The best part was the tall, gallant Texan who held her in his arms, his green eyes glittering, his captivating smile an irresistible mix of affable charm and unapologetic interest.

She laughed at something he said, for he was enchanting, this man whose eyes gleamed with a desire he did not attempt to hide. His arm tightened around her waist as he danced her effortlessly through open French doors and out into a warm, starry night. Even the moon, it seemed, was in league with his not-so-subtle seduction as he waltzed her to an intimate corner of a flagstone terrace made secluded by a vine-draped arbor, fragrantly blooming cactus and whispering crape myrtle.

When she smiled and backed away from him toward the low stone wall that encompassed the terrace, he let her go with a lingering caress, a brush of fingertip to fingertip, and a meaningful look in his eyes.

He wanted her.

Despite the warmth of the Texas night, she shivered in anticipation of the passion those green eyes promised.

"Is it wise, do you think? For us to be out here? Alone?" she asked, turning away from him and leaning into the low wall. The cool, hard stone pressing against the front of her thighs felt solid and real. Her awareness of the man and the moment sent her pulse rate soaring.

"Offhand…" his voice was meltingly low, seductively Texan, as he moved up close behind her, "I'd say it's one of the smarter moves I've made lately."

He was so close she could feel the hush of his breath, warm and intimate against her bare shoulder, so near she could sense the callused roughness of his hands even before he settled them at her waist and drew her back against him. A ripple of excitement eddied through her blood as he gently squeezed, then in a slow, smooth caress, glided his broad palms, fingers spread wide, possessively down the curve of her hip.

Her heart jumped to her throat, her breath quickened. "Mr. Walker—"

"Matt," he murmured as he lowered his mouth to her nape and his hands, in an unmistakable claim, to her outer thighs. "I think current circumstances absolutely dictate that you call me Matt."

On a sigh, she let her head fall back against his shoulder, covered his hands with hers. The heat and the hardness of him pressed against her set her on fire.

"Are all Texans this bold and sure of themselves?" she managed breathlessly.

"There's only one thing I'm sure of," he murmured and with her hands still riding his, covered her abdomen and tugged her snugly against him. His arousal pressed, provocative and brazen, against her hips. "I want you."

He turned her in his arms. His eyes smoldered with longing and lust, yet, he smiled slow and heart-meltingly sweet. Clasping her hands in his, he lifted them to his mouth, touched his lips to the fingertips of her right hand and then her left.

"You're perfect, Helena." He met her eyes in the shifting, midnight shadows. "I think I could easily fall in love with you."

He kissed her then. There beneath the West Texas moon, with the scent of the desert wafting in the air, the silk of his softly curling hair drifting through her fingers, she kissed him back. As she'd kissed no other man. Wanting him as she'd wanted no other man.

It was everything a kiss should be. Stirring yet sweet.

Hot yet unhurried. And she wanted it to go on forever. Just the two of them. Just this rich savoring of each other's mouths in the moonlight.

"Dance with me," he said against her lips and they began to move as one to the slow rhythm of the night and the hearts that beat in tandem.

The mist swirled around them, shimmering and cool, enveloping them in yet another realm, a singular world of delicious sensations and softly murmured praise. The magic continued as he waltzed her through the night to a bedroom richly appointed with sensuous satins and gossamer lace. He praised her body as he slowly undressed her. She complied willingly as he laid her naked on a down-draped bed. She invited him into her body without reservation as he whispered her name, covered her, entered her.

Like silk, he moved inside her. Like life, he gave of himself.

"You're perfect," he murmured against her brow then nuzzled heated kisses across her cheek, beneath her jaw, against the crown of her breast until she was trembling and helpless to anything but him.

"Perfect…"

A perfect pain engulfed her. So perfect and so pure she knew in an instant she was no longer dreaming. What she was feeling was real. Excruciatingly real.

She opened her eyes, jolted cruelly from the dream to predawn light, to sterile white walls, the scent of antiseptic and the awful awareness that she had been thrashing in her sleep and had slammed her left hand against the gunmetal-gray headboard of her hospital bed.

Biting back tears, she cradled her hand against her ribs and waited for the pain to subside. When, at long last, it did, she waited for sleep to reclaim her. For the magic of the dream to take her.

But sleep didn't come. Neither did the magic. Magic was for dreamers and dreamers were merely fools who found reality too difficult to bear.

"Do you have any questions about Dr. Harding's or Dr. Chambers's discharge instructions, Helena?"

Sitting up in her hospital bed, Helena smiled at Justin Webb. Not for the first time in the two months that she'd known him, she thought how lucky his new bride was to have found him. The good doctor, in addition to being handsome, had kind blue eyes. She met them steadily as the soft inflections in his voice told her his major concern had less to do with her questions than with his—specifically, the ones he didn't ask anymore because he'd given up on getting a straight answer.

A game smile in place, she shook her head. "No. I think I've got it. Watch for infections, do my mobility exercises, have a nice life."

He smiled patiently. "Helena, I'm all too familiar with the trauma a burn victim suffers when faced with the scarring and the inevitability of future reconstructive surgeries. Despite that brave front you hide behind, you're not fooling me, sweetie."

Helena's mind locked on one word and wouldn't let go. *Victim.* The word raced through her head like a brushfire that would consume her if she let it. She would not be a victim. She would not be perceived as a victim, and yet, when Justin eased a hip onto the corner of her bed it was all she could do to meet his eyes.

"The infection set you back, but you're healing well now. I know that doesn't necessarily mean any of this is easy."

For the barest of moments, she felt moisture mist her eyes. She looked quickly away before he could see it and know how right he was. It wasn't easy. It wasn't easy to know that while she would walk, she might never ski again, or ride her favorite mount—or dance with a beautiful green-eyed Texan who had haunted her dreams almost as often as the memory of the crash. But those were her problems to deal with. No one else's.

Quickly composing herself, she smiled the smile she'd perfected over the years for both the paparazzi and the public. "Justin. Darling." She patted his hand. "You worry too much. It's a—how do you Americans say it?— a piece of pie."

His grin was both indulgent and exasperated as he gently corrected her. "I believe that's piece of cake. And you're ducking the issue. Again."

She dismissed his concern with a wave of her uninjured hand. "I'm alive. I'm in one piece. And as you said, I'm healing. I'm a lucky woman. Now, I know it's part of your bedside manner to fuss, but stop it, would you? I'm fine. Really," she insisted when his grave look suggested that he suspected otherwise. She *was* fine. She was. And if she repeated it often enough, maybe she'd start to believe it.

"There are support groups," he offered after a long moment.

"Oh, please." She shook her head, smiled her most brilliant smile. "Justin. You are a kind and gifted physician. And I am a strong and healthy woman. So I've got some scarring—and this bothersome broken ankle. So I may never ski Mount Orion again. Life goes on. I'll adjust."

"I have no doubt, Helena, that you will adjust—in time. But if you would talk with someone it might speed the process. If not a support group, your family—?"

"My family," she interrupted, her smile disappearing,

"must not be bothered by this. On that point, I insist. They are not to be made aware of my condition until I'm ready to tell them."

"How can they *not* be aware? You've been front-page news for two months."

"They are not aware because they chose to believe me when I phoned to inform them that the American press is littered with sensation-seeking bottom-feeders who fabricate those horrible stories about me because they sell papers and magazines. Honestly, do *you* believe everything you read in the paper?"

She tossed her hair behind her shoulder—a purely aristocratic gesture of dismissal. "No. Of course you don't. So, of course they're not aware. My parents are on an extended tour of the Orient for their thirtieth wedding anniversary and I will not have their vacation interrupted.

"Now don't you glare at me like that, Justin. As far as my parents know, the only reason I decided to stay in the States was to see if I could cultivate interest and gather additional financial backing for one of my projects."

She graced him with another wide, winning smile—the one that had successfully opened thousands of checkbooks to the tune of millions of dollars for her numerous causes. "You Texans are known for the size of your bank accounts as well as the size of your state, is that not so? Which reminds me, darling…I've been meaning to speak to you about a donation."

"All right. All right." He held up both hands in surrender, his grin relaying both defeat and exasperation. "Message received. I'll back off. You're a big girl. You know what you can handle. Just—just call me, would you? Call anytime if you change your mind about the support group."

"Yes, Mother doctor."

"Okay. That's it." He scowled with mock seriousness and stood. "Take your smart mouth and your stubborn blue-blooded pride and do not darken these hospital doors again until I tell you you're ready for cosmetic surgery."

"Don't worry. As kind as everyone has been, I still can't get out of here fast enough."

"The timing is good then because I believe your transport is waiting."

"Gregory and Anna are here?" While Helena did not relish imposing on Princess Anna von Oberland and her husband, Gregory Hunt, she was nonetheless relieved at their offer to recuperate at their ranch, Casa Royale.

"The press got wind that you might be released today and have been camping out on the front steps. Greg and Anna are running a little interference, hoping to take some of the heat off you."

They were very gracious, the princess and her handsome husband—especially in light of the recent unpleasantness between Asterland and Princess Anna's homeland of Obersbourg. As unpleasant as it was, however, it was still more appealing to dwell on that horrible business than on the horde of reporters waiting for their first glimpse of her since the crash.

Waiting to be shocked by what they saw.

Waiting to look at her with pity in their eyes. To feed on her weakness and expose her for what she no longer was.

That, she promised herself, would never happen. They would see only what she wanted them to see. And they would not see a victim.

"Helena? Are you all right?"

"I'm fine. Fine," she insisted quickly and attempted to mask the shakiness in her voice by sitting up. "Now unless you want to see my bare backside, I'd suggest you leave me so I can get dressed." To prove she meant business, she tossed back the sheet and carefully swung her legs to the side of the bed.

"All right. I'm gone." He laughed and turned to leave.

"Justin."

Her soft voice stopped him, one hand on the door.

"Thank you. Thank you for being my friend. I'm glad it was you on call that night."

His smile was achingly endearing. "Just doing my job, ma'am."

"And I'm just doing mine, so don't forget about that donation," she reminded him, with another of those practiced smiles that she knew could charm him out of a generous contribution.

"The check's in the mail," he promised with a shake of his head, then chuckled when her playfully muttered, "Oh, I've heard that one before," chased him out the door.

Helena watched the door close slowly behind him. Alone, she let down her guard, dropped all pretense of bravery and hung her head like the coward she feared she'd become.

She'd said all the right things, made all the right noises. While Justin wasn't altogether convinced that she was all right, she felt she had convinced him that after spending most of January and all of February in the burn unit, she was bursting to get out of here.

The truth was that the thought of leaving terrified her. Yes, the isolation had been, in some ways, like a prison— but it had also been a refuge. As long as she was here, she didn't have to face the public. She didn't have to face the press.

As long as she was here, she didn't have to face the fact that she had left the world a whole, perfect person—and that she would be returning to it profoundly diminished.

* * *

A few minutes later, a light rap on the door brought Helena's head up from the simple task of buttoning her blouse. At any rate it used to be simple. Now, getting any assistance from her left hand was an exercise in pain and frustration.

Squeezing her eyes tightly, she composed herself. These resurgent and pathetic bouts of self-pity simply had to stop.

"Please come in," she called cheerily. "I'm decent. At least I'm getting there. Although you might find the air in here a bit blue."

When Anna von Oberland-Hunt walked into the room, Helena manufactured a sheepish grin for the elegant princess.

"You know, Anna, when I was a little girl, my mother was always threatening to ship me off to Australia to some obscure penal colony for foul-mouthed little hellions." She gave a self-deprecating shrug. "I'm thinking, in retrospect, it might not have been a bad plan. No doubt, if she'd been here just before you arrived, she'd have thought she should have followed through and sent me packing."

"If she were here," Anna said gently, "she would have offered to help. I'm a poor substitute, but if there's anything I can do, just say the word."

Helena shook her head to combat the renewed threat of tears that Anna's kindness fostered. "It's these cursed buttons." She sighed in exasperation. "It's rather like starting from scratch, isn't it? One two, buckle my shoe...three four, what'd they invent these blasted buttons for?"

"I'm so sorry, Helena. I should have thought of that when I selected your clothes."

"Oh, please. I already feel that I've taken horrible advantage of you. Don't make me feel worse by apologizing for your kindness."

A look that passed between them underscored Helena's gratitude for all that Anna and Greg had done—right down to retrieving her luggage from the authorities and selecting lingerie in the form of camisoles and teddies so she wouldn't have to deal with the impossible task of wrestling with a bra. Hooks, and now it seemed buttons, were currently beyond her.

Yes, she owed Anna and Gregory Hunt. The invitation they'd extended for her to stay with them was one she appreciated for both its kindness and its diplomacy. Given the strained relations between Anna's homeland of Obersbourg and Helena's of Asterland—a result of Helena's late cousin Ivan Striksky's disgraceful and failed plot to force the princess to marry him—their offer was generous beyond measure.

"It looks like you could use a little help right now," Anna offered kindly.

"A lot is more like it," Helena admitted. "And I'm past being too proud to accept it until I can manage better on my own."

If she could ever manage better. Tears welled up again. She blinked them back. *Damn and blast it.* She'd begun to think that someone had surgically removed her spine when she was under anesthetic. Worse even than dealing with her new limitations was fighting this crippling depression. She would not give in to it.

She met the princess's eyes as Anna made quick work of the pearl buttons on the dove-gray silk blouse that matched Helena's slacks. Not for the first time, she admired Anna's beauty and grace. She thought of the times that their paths had crossed. Theirs had been a passing acquaintance even though she'd often thought they would make fine friends. Now she was sure of it.

"I hope I won't have to impose on you for much more

than a month. I need to stay close to the medical complex until the graft is more stable. Then, there's this pesky thing.'' She tapped the temporary boot cast that was nearly hidden beneath her loose-legged slacks. ''This, at least I can walk in and remove from time to time until I lose it for good.''

''You have something major to look forward to then.''

''Truth to tell,'' Helena confessed, needing to take the focus away from herself, ''I am so looking forward to seeing Casa Royale. An honest-to-goodness Texas ranch. How exciting.'' Rallying another smile for Anna's benefit, she confided with a teasing lift of a brow, ''This cowboy thing is…well, it's fascinating, isn't it?''

Another rap sounded on the door.

''Ladies?'' a deep masculine voice intoned. ''How are we doing in there?''

Helena's eyes were twinkling when they met Anna's. ''Speaking of fascinating…''

Helena laughed when Anna answered her wicked grin with one of her own.

''Actually, we could use your help, Gregory.'' Anna eyed Helena's wheelchair with a dubious scowl as her husband walked into the room. ''I'm not sure how to make this thing work. Or for that matter, how to get you into it, Helena.''

''That part, I can manage,'' Helena assured them, then proved it by easing carefully off the bed. In halting steps, she maneuvered into the chair.

Greg Hunt was quick to kneel down in front of her, support her cast and adjust the leg and foot brace on the chair.

''Goodness, you're very good at that dropping to one knee business.'' Helena's eyes sparkled as she watched his dark head bent over her leg. ''Makes one wonder if Anna pulls rank on occasion and has you kneeling to the crown.''

A totally male, totally engaging grin stole across his darkly handsome face. ''A loyal subject always knows when to step and when to fetch where the princess is concerned.''

Anna looked from Greg to Helena and back to Greg. She smiled sweetly. ''Having fun?''

''Always, darling.'' He stood and dropped a kiss full of promises on her brow then turned back to Helena, who was quietly envying the love they shared. ''All set?''

''Absolutely.'' Helena told herself it wasn't a lie. She was ready to do this, and she held on to that belief right up until a racket in the hallway had them all turning their heads.

Greg strode swiftly to the door and looked outside. He turned back with a scowl. ''Looks like it's show time. The press are on the floor—and they're salivating.''

Helena had been anticipating this. She'd been preparing for it. And she'd thought she was ready. Her racing heart said she wasn't. The rush of dizziness confirmed it.

The press had tried to feed on her for her entire life. She'd always known how to handle them, had always maintained control. She'd treated them like the predators they were, using her looks to hold them at bay as a lion tamer used a whip and chair.

In a stunning moment of truth, she realized that no matter what she'd thought she could do, she couldn't hold them off now. Not in this condition. She most definitely could not control them. She wasn't that strong. To her mortification, she realized that she wasn't that brave. Without her full arsenal to draw from, they would rip her to shreds.

She met Greg's eyes, determined he'd see neither her

shame nor her fear as the noise in the hall escalated to an electric buzz in anticipation of the feeding frenzy she knew it would become.

"You know," she said, drawing on her reserves to keep her voice steady, "I really don't think I want to do this today. It's so pedestrian and, well, tacky—this spectacle they would make of something as uneventful as my release from the hospital."

Greg and Anna exchanged a concerned glance.

"I mean—can't we just make them go away somehow?" she suggested with a regal calmness her racing heart worked to undercut.

Her breath caught when the door swung open, and it suddenly seemed it was going to happen with or without her permission. She steeled herself, closed her eyes, and waited for the first verbal blow to land.

Instead of a chorus of demanding voices, one voice—a gruffly velvet, Texas drawl—rang out, clear, composed, and in total control. "It seems we've got a situation out here."

If possible, her heartbeat quickened, not with fear but with relief as she looked up and into a pair of forest-green eyes that burned so furiously and so fiercely that she would have flinched if she hadn't recognized them.

It was Matthew Walker. Her tall, green-eyed Texan. On the heels of that shock, came another. Neither her memory nor her dreams had done justice to this magnificent man in a silver-gray Stetson, slim dark slacks and crisp white shirt who had just burst back into her life like an avenging angel intent on slaying Lucifer himself if he had to.

He glanced first at Anna then at Greg before his gaze settled, with grim intensity, on her.

She didn't stop to ask him why he was here. Didn't think to question whether it was odd or out of the ordinary.

She only knew that he'd come. And because he'd come, she knew that everything would be all right.

"Well," she said, praying that neither her relief nor her panic affected her voice, "it would seem the cavalry has arrived. How wonderfully John Wayne of you." Like her tone, her smile was carefully contrived to convince everyone—including herself—that this was all one grand adventure. "So tell me, darling, how, exactly, do you intend to save the day?"

Three

The quick plan Matt had hatched to get Helena out of the hospital without being bombarded by the press was simple and effective—if reliant on a little sleight of hand. After pressing the call button to summon a nurse—who, upon hearing him out, was not only game but also excited by the prospect of a little intrigue involving a princess and the daughter of an earl—they set it in motion.

As expected, when the door to Helena's hospital room opened and Greg, with Anna by his side carrying Helena's overnight bag, wheeled the chair out into the hall, the paparazzi swarmed like piranhas around the woman bundled from head to toe in a hooded bathrobe.

Inside the room, Matt and Helena listened to the commotion. Matt watched her face and told himself he wasn't indulging in the look of her after a month of watching her from a distance. As he'd intended, she'd never been aware that he'd been standing guard. Just as she hadn't needed the extra stress of knowing she faced a potential threat added to her already difficult recovery, he hadn't needed the complications that getting to know her better would surely bring.

From the moment he'd met her, his physical reaction to her had been far too intense. His interest, much too strong. Just because he was finally face-to-face with her, just because her eyes were a deeper shade of blue than he'd remembered, the silk of her hair as lustrous as spun gold, her face and body the epitome of a heroine in a romantic novel, it didn't mean he was going to change his game plan now.

All he had to do was get her safely away from the hospital, settle her at the Hunts under the 24/7 guard he'd arranged, and he'd be back to business as usual. And yet, he couldn't take his eyes off her.

She said nothing as she sat on the edge of the bed, but the tight set of those beautiful full lips betrayed her tension. The solemn-eyed intensity of her gaze, never wavering from the closed door, spoke volumes about nerves that were strung drum-tight as the reporters' voices reached them from the hall.

"Lady Helena! Look up! Lady Helena! Over here! Give us a smile for the public who wants to know how you are."

She flinched at the sound of her name, and he couldn't help it. He reached out. Touched a hand to her shoulder, gave it a reassuring squeeze as Greg's voice boomed down the hall.

"Back off, Herkner," Greg growled at the reporter from the *American Investigator,* a sleazy tabloid that put the other rags to shame in the exploitation department. "Give the lady a break. And give the other patients on the floor

a break, too. Let us get her out of the building and she'll
give you a few words and a chance to shoot some photos.

"Or don't back off," Greg baited, the dare in his voice
unmistakable, "and we'll let the ER docs practice a little
triage on your ugly face. Your call, of course."

Matt looked toward the closed door, very much aware
of the history between Willis Herkner and Greg Hunt. The
reporter had hounded Anna during the Striksky affair. Obviously, Greg held a grudge. More obviously, Herkner was
hamburger if he tested those particular waters.

When the racket quieted to a hushed din, telling Matt
his plan was working and Greg and Anna were leading the
press from the floor, he turned back to Helena.

She was pale and shaken and trying valiantly to keep
herself together.

He hunkered down in front of her. "Hey…you okay?"

She worked over-hard to gather her composure and
grace him with a look that tried to make a lie of the fact
that she was far from all right. "Of course, darling," she
said in that cool, regal tone that dismissed his concern as
unnecessary. "It's just such a bother, isn't it?"

"And then some," he agreed, trying to get a read on
her, knowing there was more going on behind those brilliant blue eyes than she wanted him to see.

"Look," she said, all starch and breeding and a bit of
impatient prima donna that didn't quite ring true, "I don't
know why you're here. And frankly, I don't care. Just get
me out of here. Please," she added with enough entreaty
that he knew she wasn't as blasé about all of this as she'd
like him to think.

He tipped his fingers to his hat brim and because he felt
she needed one, he gave her a reassuring smile. "At your
service, my lady."

She smiled then, too. A real smile, not one he suspected

she'd used on the public to hide everything from boredom to pain to fear.

"What's next?" she asked after a steadying breath.

"What's next is that we sneak you out the rear entrance without catching anyone's attention."

And that was going to be no easy feat. He'd been afraid that her release would come to this. The media circus it created wasn't the worst of it. The worst of it was that her visibility increased her vulnerability. He wasn't about to give anyone but the people he trusted access to her.

All he needed to do was transport her safely out of the hospital and deliver her to the Hunts. Greg was a fellow Cattleman's Club member and Matt knew she'd be safe with him and Anna at their ranch until the mystery behind the jewel theft and Riley's murder was cleared up, and he was certain she was out of danger.

She'd also be out of his line of sight at the Hunts'. Maybe then, she'd be out of his mind, too. Right, and a cactus didn't have needles. Regardless of where she was in proximity to where he was, he was afraid he'd be seeing those big baby blues for a long time to come.

He drew a deep breath, got back to business. They had to get moving. He eyed her cast. "Can you walk in that thing?"

"I suppose that would depend on your definition of walk. Hobble might better describe it," she admitted with something close to an apology in her eyes.

He stood. "Hobble's not going to cut it, I'm afraid." He scrubbed a palm over his jaw, gave her a considering once-over. "So we improvise."

Careful of her injuries, he scooped her from the bed and into his arms. She felt good there. Too good. So good, he knew he had to do something to get his mind off the sudden, unplanned intimacy.

''Whoa,'' he teased and settled her more securely against his chest. ''Not exactly a featherweight, are you?''

Actually she was a sleek and silky armful. His heart kicked into overdrive—not so much from the exertion as from the softness of her breast snuggled hot and full against his chest. It was not the reaction of choice, but he sure as hell wasn't going to dwell on it. What he was going to do was make the lady relax. Another one of those smiles wouldn't be too tough to take either.

With staged effort, he shifted her higher in his arms and made a big show of being staggered by her slight weight.

''It's the cast,'' she assured him with a tight little scowl and looped her left arm around his neck. ''And the case,'' she added, referring to the clear plastic case she cradled in her lap that appeared to be filled with the home-going medical supplies.

He grunted for good measure. ''If you say so.''

''Oh, for pity's sake, get over it. I thought you cowboy types were supposed to be big and strong and well... heroic.'' She glared down that titled little nose of hers in such a regal, aristocratic attempt to look huffy it was all he could do not to laugh.

''Begging your pardon, Lady Helena, but I've bull-dogged steers that weighed less than you.''

She forced a tight smile, but her eyes held absolutely no trace of amusement. ''That just makes my day, doesn't it? I've been compared to a lot of things but never live-stock. How charming.''

He grinned, but, still aware that she was far more nervous about this business than she was letting on, made sure she understood she could count on him. ''It's going to be all right. You can trust me, okay?''

When those expressive eyes held his gaze, and she softly murmured, ''I do,'' a long-repressed Tarzan gene made him want to beat his chest and carry her off to some vine-covered treetop hideaway. Since, for more reasons than one, that wasn't an option, he gave her a quick wink instead and headed for the door.

The hall was devoid of reporters as they slipped cautiously out of the room. He shook off the floor nurse's offer of another wheelchair and carried Helena to the bank of elevators marked Staff Only. Once at ground level, he negotiated a series of twists and turns as he carried her through the hallways to the rear exit.

"You seem to be rather good at this skulking business." She tightened her arm around his neck. "Makes one wonder if there might be a bit of a shady past one might need to get a bit nervous about."

He ignored the warmth of her, the woman scent of her and concentrated on putting one foot in front of the other. "Old American saying—*One* shouldn't look a gift rescuer in the mouth."

She gave a delicate little sniff. "Oh, by all means, rescue away. You'll get no resistance from me."

He smiled. "Here's where we see just how good a sleuth I really am." He rounded the last corner and the rear exit came into sight. "It's show time. Cross your fingers, countess. We're going to make a run for it."

"I'm not a countess," she said breathlessly as he shouldered through the revolving door and sprinted down the steps.

"Close enough." He looked both ways and made a break for the parking lot. "My pocket," he said, striding along the asphalt. "See if you can fish my keys out of my pocket."

Bad idea, he realized belatedly as her small, seeking right hand stole down, felt around for his trouser pocket opening and finally slipped inside. He suppressed a groan as the warmth of her fingers connected with his hip, then his thigh, then, oblivious to what she was doing to him, accidentally brushed something else that threatened to stand at immediate attention.

With steel will, he ignored all the pulse-altering groping going on south of his belt buckle. At least he tried to.

Way too late—or way too soon—she gave a victorious tug and pulled the keys free.

"I got them."

"Thank you, Jesus, Joseph and Mary," he muttered through gritted teeth, and sincerely hoped she hadn't noticed what she had unintentionally done to him.

"Click the lock release."

Her slender right hand gripped the keyless remote, the tip of her index finger poised on the red button. "This one?"

"That's the—" horns and sirens bleated into the relative stillness in absurdly loud and frantic blasts "—alarm," he finished unnecessarily.

Wide blue eyes met his with startled comprehension. "Oops."

He glanced over his shoulder to see what kind of attention they'd attracted—and caught her expression instead.

She looked a little mortified and a lot fearful of getting caught. What could he do but smile at her and try to make that look go away?

"It's not a problem, okay? It'll just make our getaway more interesting. I'm going to set you down now. Can you support your weight on one leg for a second?"

"Considering that in your estimation I weigh roughly the same as a Hereford," she enunciated over the irritating drone of the alarm, "it will be a challenge, but I'll give it my all."

He hugged her then. He hadn't meant to. He knew she

would bristle right up at the notion, but she was just so darned cute with her upper-crust attitude and her put-upon pride that he acted before he thought, and then it was too late to do anything but make nice.

She merely blinked at him, big and bright and, if he chose to believe it, a bit shyly.

With another glance over his shoulder, he relieved her of the keys, neutralized the alarm, and hit the lock release. "In you go." He quickly opened the passenger door.

Very carefully, he helped her get comfortable then stowed her bag in the back seat. "Do we need to put that foot up?"

"It's fine. Let's just get out of here before they figure out they've been fooled."

"I'm with you on that one."

He sprinted around the vehicle, jumped in and slammed the door behind him. "Fasten your seat belt and hang on to your hat. We may be in for a wild ride."

A long beat of silence passed. "Well," she said quietly. "I'd like to do both. The problem is, I don't have a hat. And at the moment, I'm afraid that seat-belt issue is beyond me, too."

One hand on the wheel, the other on the ignition, he glanced her way—then realized his insensitivity. She couldn't fasten the belt.

From the moment he'd walked into her room, he'd not only been profoundly aware of her as a woman, but he'd sensed a self-consciousness about her hand that he suspected she'd never admit to. He'd tried not to stare, but now he did and fully realized what she was up against. Her left hand was covered in a snug, protective mesh glove, her fingers extended at a stiff, unnatural angle.

When she cupped her injured hand protectively with her right, he could have kicked himself.

"I'm sorry."

Her chin notched up a fraction. "You have nothing to be sorry for. It's not you who can't manage this contraption."

No. It wasn't him who couldn't manage, although there were a few things giving him his own share of trouble at the moment. One of them was that kissable mouth of hers. It was lush and full and just begging for someone to kiss her and make it all better.

He couldn't make it better though. And kissing her was out of the question. His job was to protect her. If he didn't get her out of here soon, he wasn't even going to manage that.

"May I?" he offered gently.

She stared through the windshield. Gave a clipped nod.

Her breath caught—he swore it did—when he twisted at the hip and leaned toward her. By sheer force of will, he kept his gaze from connecting with hers as he reached across her body for the seat-belt strap—and then *he* was the one struggling for an even breath as the soft whisper of hers feathered against his jaw.

Her generous breasts rose and fell beneath the silk of her blouse as he fumbled with the belt like a horny teenager before finally managing to buckle her in. In silence, he absorbed it all, the scent of her, the heat of her, and the pride that she was having a difficult time clinging to. Then there was the very obvious fact that she wasn't wearing a bra, and his suspicion that something other than the mild March chill had caused the tips of her nipples to harden like tiny buttons and strain against soft gray silk.

He eased away, far too aware of the absence of all that delicious heat no longer snuggled against him. And way too willing to taste those full, lush lips.

Squared up behind the steering wheel, he thumbed back

his hat, rolled his shoulders. Well. That was interesting. And stupid. There was no way he was going in that direction with her. For a lot of reasons. None of them having to do with how vulnerable she looked. Most of them having to do with lessons learned about high-maintenance women. Women who lived, breathed and required a lifestyle that was well within his means, but not within his disposition to provide.

Without a word, he shifted into first gear and eased out of the lot just as his cell phone rang. Relieved to have the diversion, he opened the console that ran between the bucket seats. Snagging the phone, he punched the button on the second ring.

"Walker."

"Matt. It's Greg. I take it you made it without incident?"

Matt let out a breath he'd probably been holding since he'd made the mistake of looking into eyes so blue it made him think of bluebonnets under a summer sky. Without incident? Not quite.

"Close enough." He hooked a left turn at the corner of Market and Fifteenth. "We're headed for Casa Royale now."

"Sorry, but that's got to be a negative. Once the troops figured out they'd been hoodwinked, they decided to divide and conquer. Half of them tore back into the hospital. The rest are following Anna and me to the ranch. You bring Helena here right now and they'll hound her like a wolf pack."

Matt swore under his breath.

"What is it?" Despite her attempt to conceal it, enough tension to string a guitar hummed through Helena's breathless question. "What's wrong?"

He glanced from the street to her face. If possible, those

telling eyes of hers had grown bigger and more apprehensive. It was looks like those that made him forget why he didn't want to get involved with her.

"It's all right," he assured her and returned his attention to Greg. "Okay. We regroup. Any ideas?"

"I don't see too many options except the obvious. You're going to have to take Helena to High Stakes for a few days until this settles down."

Like it or not, Matt didn't see any options either.

"Anna and I will lead them around by the nose for a while. Give you a little more time. We'll be back in touch, okay?"

"Bet on it," Matt said with certainty and disconnected.

"What's happened?"

He glanced her way, then back at the street. What had happened was that his perfect plan to tuck Helena out of sight and out of mind had just blown up in his face like a shotgun with a jammed barrel.

"The press. Half of them are still looking for you at the hospital—the rest are following Greg and Anna like a jet trail. They probably figure you'll eventually end up at Casa Royale."

A long silence passed before she uttered a very controlled, "I see."

He glanced her way again, trying to read her reaction. "I'm sorry, Helena. But it looks like you're going to be my guest for a few days, until they back off. I hope you don't mind."

Her eyes widened a bit with an emotion he couldn't quite decipher before she looked away. "I don't mind." Her voice was very soft. "I don't mind at all."

Well, he was in for it now, wasn't he? Matt thought as he headed down the final mile to High Stakes. He'd gone and brought the countess—or whatever she was—to his home turf.

He drummed his fingers on the steering wheel. There was nothing to do about it for now. Until the timing was right to transport her to the Hunts', he'd simply have to be the gentleman his mother raised him to be and offer her a safe and secluded harbor. This didn't have to turn into anything more than what it was. He was her protector. It ended there.

Right. And he didn't want her in his bed so bad he ached with it.

It didn't make any sense, and yet, there it was. For the past two months he'd been able to keep his unwanted attraction for her, if not at bay, at least in check. In the last hour things seemed to have snowballed way out of control. Maybe Justin was right. Maybe he was suffering from sleep deprivation. He couldn't remember the last time he'd caught more than two or three uninterrupted hours of shut-eye.

He rotated his head on his neck, then rolled his shoulders. What he had to remember was that while Helena seemed vulnerable now, she would recover. Sure she was hurting—even though she tried to hide it behind that subject-to-peasant look that did little to disguise just how fragile she was.

So, he would be compassionate. He would be considerate. And all the time, he would remember who she was, what she was, and that in a few days she'd be gone.

And still, he wanted her.

Okay. He was a big boy. He could deal with it. He understood lust. It was clean and honest and totally independent of emotion. Emotion. There was the crux of the problem, now, wasn't it? He'd seen too much at the hospital. Witnessed, a little too often, her pain. And he figured he understood, a little too well, how important it was to her to hide it.

She was a great pretender. He suspected much of who she was was based on pretense and figured she must be digging deep right about now to make sure no one knew how frightened she really was.

Maybe that's the difference he sensed between Helena and Jena. When his ex-wife had been unhappy, everyone had known it. And everyone had suffered.

He'd made himself think about Jena a lot lately. Made himself remember why he needed to fight this attraction to Helena. Jena had taught him a valuable lesson about high-maintenance women. The Earl of Orion's daughter might be a charming and beautiful rose of a woman, but, like Jena, she would never be a desert rose.

Eyes dead ahead, he flexed his fingers on the wheel. That's why he knew better than to even think—however abstractly—about getting involved with Helena. A high-ticket woman like her ladyship here and ranch life would mix about as well as hurricanes and hand grenades.

He let out a deep breath. And got a slippery grip on some much-needed perspective. Reality check: he wasn't marrying Helena Reichard. He was just giving her a place to stay. Temporarily. A few days, tops. For the next couple of days, he couldn't think about the sparks that had flashed between them that night as they'd danced. He couldn't dwell on this notion that there had been something about her—a reckless spontaneity, an honest charm. And he'd forget that he'd sensed an interest she'd returned, along with an undeniable awareness that she had been as baffled—and as shaken—by the attraction as he'd been.

So the rush of desire he'd felt when he'd waltzed her across the room had been as potent and as pure as his private blend of bourbon that Riley had always made sure was stocked in the club's bar just for him.

Riley. His thoughts sobered abruptly. Riley was dead. The diamond was still missing. And the woman looking so lost and so lovely as she stared through the windshield was in need of nothing from him but his protection.

It all came back to that. And despite all of his rationalizations, he wished to hell that he were a little more upset about the fact that she was going to be with him, and not with the Hunts.

Just until the press backed off, he reminded himself staunchly. Then he'd escort her royal-whatever-she-was to Greg and Anna's, and he'd get on with his life. A life he liked fine just the way it was, thank you very much.

No sooner had he grounded himself in those absolutes and pulled into the drive at High Stakes than another thought hit him double-barrel.

He groaned. "Lois."

Speaking of hurricanes and hand grenades.

Beside him, her face pale and pinched with fatigue and what he strongly suspected was pain she'd never admit to, Helena turned her curious gaze to his. "Lois?"

He blew out a breath, resettled his Stetson. How did he explain Lois? "Lois is my…housekeeper. Sort of. Ah, look. I should prepare you. Lois is, well, Lois is—"

"Your lover?" she concluded with a stiff little arch of her brow. "I assure you, Mr. Walker, your personal life is no concern of mine. I apologize deeply for any incon—"

"Hold it. Just…just hold it, okay?" Both amused and intrigued by a reaction that smacked of, for lack of a better word, jealousy, he studied her china-doll profile. Jealousy? No way. He wasn't even going to go there.

"Lois is *not* my lover." He couldn't help it. A chuckle slipped out. "And she'll offer to wash your mouth out with soap for even uttering such a suggestion. Lois is, well, she's more like a fixture at High Stakes. She's also a little gruff sometimes. She means well so don't let her bull-headedness and snorting bother you.''

''Bullheaded? Snorting? How interesting. Is this a Texas thing—all these livestock references?''

When she gazed down her patrician little nose and gave him that look again—the one that suggested she might have had a little silver bell in her possession at some point in her life and hadn't been shy about using it—he reminded himself why he couldn't find it adorable. Why he needed to find it reaffirming.

Still, another grin slipped past his guard. ''Why yes, ma'am, I reckon you could say it is,'' he allowed, pouring on the Texas drawl for her benefit.

He pulled to a stop in front of the ranch house and cut the motor. One look at her face and his smile disappeared. He'd been so busy convincing himself why he needed to keep his head on straight where Helena was concerned, he'd momentarily forgotten just how difficult this was for her.

She'd endured a devastating plane crash, she'd spent two painful months in the hospital recovering, and now she was stuck with him in a strange place, in a difficult situation, and she had yet to utter one word of complaint.

''You look exhausted,'' he said, surveying the pale vi-olet bruises of fatigue beneath her eyes. ''Let's get you inside and get you comfortable.''

Helena was too tired to even respond. And too over-whelmed with thoughts of the strange twist of fate that had landed her, quite literally, in Matthew Walker's arms. She tried not to think about the effect those arms had on her. Of their powerful strength, of their heat. Of how easy it would be to become dependent on them.

She tried not to think about how wonderful it felt to be held by him. She definitely didn't want to think about the swift, uncontrollable flash of jealousy she'd experienced when she'd thought he had a lover waiting for him.

Feeling her cheeks flush red, she forced herself to think, instead, about the drive out here and of what she'd seen so far of High Stakes. This was the Texas she had read about and imagined. Long stretches of endless, barren plains. Tumbleweed and sagebrush, gnarly-branched trees that Matthew had told her were mesquite. Cactus and oil derricks dotting the horizon for farther than the eye could see.

Amid all that stark and somehow barren beauty, Matthew's home settled like a sparkling jewel upon a carpet of velvet green. Heavily influenced by Spanish architecture, the two-story adobe building that was the main house glittered like a golden crown in the midday sun. Several smaller outbuildings—at least two of them residences—and three large horse barns flanked the main house, forming a compact community of sorts.

She blinked, refocused her gaze on Matthew's long, sure strides as he rounded the front of the vehicle then opened the passenger door. Without meeting her eyes, he released her seat belt.

"Ready?" he asked politely.

Too politely to suit her. It was as if he'd intentionally distanced himself. She wasn't sure why his sudden formality upset her, but it did. So much so that she gave him that look again, the one that he seemed to find so amusing.

"Let's see if I have mastered the local—dialect. One moo for yes, two for no, would that be correct?"

He gave her exactly the reaction she'd wanted. A slow, enchanting grin started at one corner of his mouth and spread like a sunrise across his very remarkable face. And when he topped it off with a low and husky, "Moo," little rivers of heat trickled through her blood and sent a wild, tingling sensation chasing in their wake.

How very fascinating. After two months of feeling little but loneliness and pain, Matthew Walker had an infectious way of making her feel alive. It was exhilarating and a little frightening how easily he could make her forget, if even for a moment, what she'd been through, what she still faced.

"Has anyone ever suggested that you've got quite the sassy mouth on you for a countess?" he asked as she wrapped her arms around his neck and he lifted her carefully out of the vehicle.

"I keep trying to tell you. I'm not a countess. I'm the daughter of the countess. That merely makes me—"

"—one of the prettiest little heifers seen around these parts in a month of Sundays," he drawled, his tongue so deep in his cheek she was surprised he hadn't bitten it off.

She looked away so he couldn't see her smile. Because really, she didn't want to be so taken with him. But he was such a nice man, this Matthew Walker, she thought, as she nestled in his strong arms and he carried her toward the house. She'd thought as much many times since the night they'd met. And he was too handsome for his own good. Or hers.

She allowed herself the luxury, though, of studying the dramatic lines of his profile as he concentrated on carrying her across an intricately laid flagstone walkway. His face was tanned and smoothly shaven, although the shadow of a heavy beard was noticeable on his lean cheeks and impossibly square jaw.

Dark brows perfectly showcased striking green eyes that had the most fascinating crinkles at their corners. The fine lines would have revealed his penchant for those quick, ready grins had she not already witnessed them firsthand.

Complementing the package were long, lean cheeks, deeply creased with the most amazing grooves that framed his mouth like parentheses when he smiled...as he so often did. His nose was blade-straight and bold, a mirror of his character that she was beginning to know, perhaps, a bit better than was wise.

This close, she could see the way his dark hair softly curled at ̲ his nape. This close, she could see the jump of his pulse just beneath his jaw, smell the scent of him the heat of the Texas sun had unleashed to send her senses reeling.

His was no sophisticated, designer fragrance manufactured to intimidate in the boardroom or entice in the bedroom. But he did entice, just by smelling like a man. Like honest sweat. Like Texas desert. Like a man who worked with horses and leather yet knew how to touch a woman's heart with something as simple and as fanciful as a softly murmured, "Moo."

He was nothing remotely like the men she was used to. Men so polished and pompous they wouldn't know how to tease or take a joke if their title depended on it. Or men so inane and intent on advancing their social or financial position they reminded her of fluttery little drones hovering around the queen bee.

Matthew wouldn't hover around any man. Or woman. And he couldn't, she reminded herself with a grave certainty, be interested in her. Not now.

Once she could have turned his head.

Once when she was strong and whole.

Now, he was simply being kind.

And that knowledge was, perhaps, even more painful than the injuries that had yet to fully heal.

Four

"**Y**ou couldn't have picked up a phone?"

Eyes wide, her fatigue momentarily forgotten, Helena clung to Matthew's neck and simply stared. He still held her in his arms just outside his front door, facing off with approximately four feet eleven inches of round, plump curves and snow-white hair. Age-spotted fists—one of them clutching a wooden spoon—propped on apron-covered hips, mustached upper lip puckered into a condemning scowl, the pint-sized Attila the Hun laid into over six feet of lean, muscled male as if she actually thought she could intimidate him.

Evidently, she could, Helena realized incredulously, if the flush spreading slowly upward from under the collar of Matthew's white shirt was any indication. His reaction was fascinating—and utterly enchanting.

"Lois—" he warned reasonably, and hefted Helena a little higher in his arms.

"Don't you take and Lois me, you inconsiderate little pup. A phone call. Was it too much to expect? You bring me home a countess and you couldn't take and pick up that fancy portable phone and call? Nooo. I had to hear it from the neighbors. Well, at least that Hunt boy knows his manners and called to let me know you were on your way. Your poor momma. She would faint dead away with embarrassment if she heard about this. Dead away."

"I'm sorry, Lois."

"Sorry, he says." With a quick jerk of her shoulders, she made a loud, snorting sound. "Why, I've a notion to take and put my spoon to your backside, Mister, and don't you think for a minute I can't still do it."

"Lois," he interrupted, interjecting a cautious, albeit pleading note of authority into his tone. "This is Lady Helena Reichard. She's going to be our guest for a few days."

Lois merely snorted again. "And what kind of heathens must she take and think we are? Letting her arrive unannounced. No room made ready for her."

"There are half a dozen bedrooms in this house—surely we can find one that will work. That is, if you'll ever let us in," he enunciated pointedly.

With a disgruntled huff, Lois backed way from the door, then turned to Helena. She made a jerky, self-conscious little curtsey, a welcome smile in place.

"Lady Helena, please excuse Matthew's unforgivable manners. He's been taught better, he truly has. He's a good boy at heart, but spoiled, I'm sorry to say and doesn't know the proper way to take and treat a lady."

"Lois," Matthew warned as he walked through the spacious foyer and into a graceful sunlit living area flanked by high arching windows and vaulted ceilings. "Do I need to remind you who—eeyow!" he yelped as the sharp rap of Lois's wooden spoon connected soundly with his backside.

"Put her down before you drop her," Lois commanded, her tone inviting no arguments. "Poor dear. Manhandled by the likes of a clumsy cowboy. And her a countess and all."

"She's not a countess," he ground out as he carefully settled Helena on a cream-colored linen sofa. "She's the daughter of a countess."

"And so pale and pretty she is. You're tired, aren't you, dear? And probably thirsty. Matthew—take and fetch some iced tea for the countess. Sugar, dear?"

Helena blinked from Matthew to Lois and shook her head.

"Two spoons in mine, please," Lois ordered. "And lots of ice."

Helena watched, transfixed, as the glare Matt directed at Lois gave way to a slow shake of his head and a resigned grin.

"Yes, ma'am. Anything you say, ma'am. Right away, ma'am." His gaze on Helena, he touched his fingers to his hat brim, rolled his eyes and headed out of the room.

Helena watched him go, then gingerly turned her attention back to Lois who had seated herself regally on a matching sofa that faced Helena across a low pine table.

"Now, dear," Lois murmured with a warmth in her voice that was totally at odds with the irritation she'd shown Matthew, "take and tell me all about yourself."

Moonlight danced across the bleached pine floor of the south-facing room that was her bedroom. The clean, classic lines of mission oak furniture filled the room, from the massive armoire to the king-size bed. Intricately woven rugs in sand and mauve and the softest blues and greens were scattered over the gleaming floor, draped over the bedside tables, hung stunningly as artwork on the oatmeal-colored walls.

Helena sat in an upholstered rocker at a wall of floor-to-ceiling windows, watching the shimmer of distant stars compete with the stark beauty of an ink-black heaven.

She'd never seen such a wide, spacious sky.

And she'd never felt smaller or more insignificant than she did in this vast Texas night. It was humbling. And unsettling.

Equally disconcerting was how, at this point in her life, she had ended up here. In this condition. In Matthew Walker's home.

Tell me all about yourself.

Lois's words came back to her as if she'd just spoken them. She'd been shocked by the question. No one but Lois had ever asked her to do that before. Everyone had always known who she was. Until two months ago, she'd thought *she'd* known who she was.

Tell me all about yourself.

To her utter horror, she'd looked blankly at Lois, and she hadn't known what to say. She'd realized that although she had tried to deny it, the accident had had a profound effect on her life. She honestly didn't know who she was anymore. In that stunning moment of discovery, she wondered if she ever had. She'd always been her daddy's darling girl. She'd been the world's beautiful Lady Helena. She didn't know how to be anything else.

But wasn't there more to her than that? Shouldn't there be more?

As she sat alone reflecting, she realized that her life to date had been one series of obligatory performances after another. Her selection as a member of the Asterland delegation sent to Texas to smooth the politically troubled waters between Obersbourg and the United States that her cousin Ivan had riled, was just one in a line of many obligations she'd been called upon to fulfill.

And now, because of that fateful trip her life, as she'd known it, was changed forever.

She looked through the window at the darkness of night and the flat terrain beyond. Who would have conceived a simple diplomatic function would have brought her to this juncture in her life?

She was in Texas. Even more interesting, she was with Matthew Walker, a man she had found intriguing at first sight. A man she had despaired over leaving before getting to know him better. It seemed a twisted sort of irony that it was Matthew who had walked back into her life today. She had wanted to see him again—but not like this. Never like this.

A soft knock at the door brought her head around and her heart racing. Without conscious thought, she tucked her left hand into the folds of her borrowed robe. ''Come in.''

When Matthew walked into the room, a little shiver of awareness rippled through her body. It was pointless to react to him this way. Before the accident, maybe. But not now. Along with certain thoughts she couldn't control, however, neither could she control her reaction to him.

It was the night. It was her memory of the way he'd held her in his arms—his scent that tugged at her senses and made her so keenly aware of him as a man—and of the woman she had once been.

He was strong and yet gentle, and the indulgence he'd shown Lois reaffirmed that he was also kind. All were qualities hard to resist in a man—were there a need to resist him.

As he stepped into the room, she searched his face for

a sign that he might still feel this attraction, too—then fought an unreasonable disappointment when she saw only cordial concern as he walked toward her.

"Are you settled in?" he asked as he extended one of two glasses of deep red wine he'd brought with him.

Too aware of the tingling sensation when their fingers brushed, she murmured a soft, "Yes, thank you," and became mesmerized by the contrast of the dark tan of his skin against the milky whiteness of his shirt.

He'd unbuttoned the top three buttons, rolled his sleeves to his elbows. Soft brown curls peeked from the open placket at his chest, dusted strong forearms heavily corded with sinew and deeply set veins.

At the Cattleman's Club gala, he'd worn an ink-black Stetson with his western-cut tux. Today, his hat had been silver. The first time she'd seen him hatless was at dinner tonight. In a hat, he was stunning. Without one, he was devastating. He'd taken her breath away. Now here, in the soft light of the bedroom, he made her heart do strange, frantic things beneath her breast.

All those thick, brown curls were a little wild, a little unruly, much as she suspected the man could be if he ever let her see anything of himself but engaging charm and gentle teasing. On another man, those soft curls might have looked effeminate. He wasn't another man. She was struck again by the realization that he was like no man she'd ever met.

At the moment, he looked contemplative and sober—and very tired—as he stood there, the silence stretching for so long she felt a need to fill it.

She drew a steadying breath. "What I've seen of High Stakes is wonderful, Matthew. And this room...it's right out of a little European girl's fantasy of the Wild West. Over all, it's quite an adventure."

His green eyes watched her, his expression unreadable and somehow disconcerting, as if he could see right through her. Right down to a fear that had settled marrow deep and that she tried to hide behind inane conversations and regal airs.

Feeling herself flush, she looked away, sipped, then savored her wine. "I can't tell you how delicious this tastes after two months without so much as the sight of a cool, chilled bottle."

"I'm glad you approve."

"I do. Very much."

Another silence settled, one that would be too easy to get lost in, just as she could get lost in the color of his eyes.

"Lois, well, she's quite—unusual, isn't she?" she offered, not only to break the silence but because Lois intrigued her.

His features softened. "I did warn you."

"Yes. Yes, you did. I wish she didn't feel the need to curtsey. I've told her it's absolutely unnecessary."

"You can tell her anything you want," he said, a smile in his voice, "but if Lois has it in her mind she's going to do it, it's going to happen. Necessary or not, she'll play out her little fantasy her way. I haven't seen her this excited since my sisters' weddings."

She tilted her head, studied him. "You're very fond of her, aren't you?"

"Have to be." He swirled the wine, then arched a brow over the top of the glass. "She'd take and tan my hide if I wasn't."

She smiled into his laughing eyes and knew without doubt that if she was going to survive this episode with her heart intact, she needed some distance from all that charisma, all that sex appeal. Long term, her eventual move to the Hunts' would help. Short term, she was in a little trouble. She couldn't simply get up and walk away from him—not without drawing attention to her limp. Right or wrong, she felt a little too raw, a lot too sensitive to let him see her struggle that way.

"I think, perhaps, it's more than that," she said, choosing the option available at the moment and trying to focus on Lois.

He tugged on his ear. "Yeah. It's more than that. She's cantankerous and bossy and—"

"—and as bullheaded as oh, say, a Hereford?" she suggested making them both smile.

"Yeah," he agreed, his voice low and warm and amused. "As bullheaded as that."

She felt that damnable heat flush her cheeks again as he watched her with intimate eyes and an interest she couldn't let herself believe.

"Well," she continued, looking to the window, then to her wine, "she was very sweet to me."

When he sat down in a matching chair that faced hers, she felt too much elation and not enough dread over the fact that he appeared to be settling in for a while.

"She's very taken with you. I hope she didn't wear you out."

"No. Oh, no. It was like talking to my aunt Amelia, the dowager duchess. They're both crusty, opinionated icons. I love that about them. The eccentricity, the forthrightness. It's refreshing."

"Most of the time," he agreed with another smile. "Lois takes pride in proclaiming that she and her husband, Frank, have been with the family since before I was even a sparkle in my daddy's eye. Frank's seventy-five and still riding fence. And Lois—well, Lois is still running the show at High Stakes. They both could have retired years ago but since Lois gets all huffy and drags out her spoon when the *R* word is mentioned, we just keep the status quo—if for no other reason, to keep the peace.''

"And because you love them," she concluded, noting that particular emotion was clear in his voice.

"Yes," he admitted. "Because I love them."

The honesty of his emotions also played across his face. How refreshing. And how uncomplicated. Just as the man seemed uncomplicated, she thought, watching him. But was he really? She suspected not. She suspected that there was much more to Matthew Walker than charismatic smiles and gentle wit. And she wished it were possible for her to get to know him well enough to find out. Since she would be leaving in a short time, there was little point in thinking along those lines. And yet, she did. She did want to know him better.

Two months ago, she wouldn't have hesitated at a little aggressive flirtation to finesse the information out of him. Two months ago, she'd been confident that he would have responded. Now, she was confident of nothing. Especially her own physical appeal.

He lifted his glass to his lips again then watched her with quiet eyes as another silence enveloped the room. "How are you feeling?"

"I'm fine," she insisted quickly when he sat back in the chair and, with a tilt of his head, relayed his uncertainty.

"It's very beautiful, your High Stakes," she continued evasively, needing to steer the subject away from herself, needing to steer her thoughts away from that unfamiliar uncertainty that had become her constant, unwanted companion. "And very…" she hesitated, sought the right word, finally decided on, "Texas."

Their eyes met, held for the longest of moments before

he looked out the window, cleared his throat. "You'll be more comfortable when we get you resettled at the Hunts'. Casa Royale is a sprawling one-level hacienda. You won't have the stairs to deal with there."

She blinked. Lowered her head. Well, there was a preemptory goodbye if she'd ever heard one. His statement shouldn't have felt so much like a blow, but it did. The thought of leaving shouldn't have felt so much like disappointment either, but there it was, teaming up with everything else that seemed determined to undercut her confidence. Of course he wanted to be rid of her. She was a disruption to his life.

She drew a bracing breath, accepting that she'd faced many disappointments in the past two months and it was time to get used to it.

"I'm sorry, Matthew—about the stairs. I'd never forgive myself if you put your back out carrying me up and down them."

Green eyes glittering, he gave her a slow, assessing once-over. "If I can't manage a lightweight like you, there's not a lot of hope."

Oh, those eyes. Oh, that look. Did he have any idea what it did to a woman? Yes. She supposed he did, and yet, there was such a gentle spontaneity to his reply that she forgave him for it.

"Lightweight? Lightweight—steer?" she suggested, attempting to keep her voice and, she hoped, the mood, light.

Another slow, lazy grin shot a spike of searing heat straight to her heart. "You don't forget much, do you?"

"Mind like a steel trap."

He nodded, giving the point to her. "I may have exaggerated a bit."

Since she, herself, was a master of innocuous flirtation, she knew exactly how little import to attach to that smile.

She'd let many an ardent admirer down with one just like it, so she understood that he'd meant nothing by it. And that's what hurt the most.

She also understood that he'd have been dismayed to know that his lack of interest cut like the twist of a knife. So, she'd just make sure he'd never know.

"Well, I do thank you for that." Despite the disappointment, she gave in to her spontaneous need to return his smile.

It was just so easy, that smile. It sort of unfurled—slow and sexy and sincere and by the time it was full blown, she couldn't help but react to it.

"In any event," she continued, determined to mask the disappointment that was far too real and altogether defeating, "it really wasn't necessary for you to carry me. I could have managed the stairs. I *need* to manage stairs."

"And you will—in time," he assured her. "Now, I want an honest answer this time. How are you feeling? Truth."

She looked at her wine. Looked at him. "The truth is that it feels so very good to have that cast off for a while."

He looked down, focused on her bare feet peeking out from beneath the long robe. She saw him swallow, let out a breath…and for the briefest of moments, let herself believe that she saw something more intense than concern. Something that hovered near awareness. Whatever it was, it made her heartbeat quicken.

"Is that wise—to take it off, I mean?"

Her heart still hadn't settled when she decided she'd only wished for something that wasn't there. "Yes, actually. I think Dr. Chambers has me wearing it more for precaution now. He assures me I can get rid of it completely in a couple of days if the X rays look good."

"And it's really not bothering you?"

She shrugged, unwilling to admit to the pain. "Oh, it throbs a bit."

"You need to get it up."

"I will. Soon."

Another small silence fell, one that was long enough for her to finally form the question that had been hovering in the back of her mind since he'd stormed into her hospital room this afternoon like an avenging angel. "Matthew, how did you happen to be at the hospital today?"

It was his turn to look into his glass before meeting her eyes again. "Actually, I'd come to talk to Justin. Thought as long as I was there, I'd stop in and say hello."

Something flashed in his expression before he shifted his shoulders, tipped back his glass then averted his gaze to the window. She'd always been fairly astute at reading body language. And Matthew's body was speaking to her. The signals he was sending suggested he wasn't being truthful. She couldn't imagine why he'd felt he had to lie—unless he thought they both needed him to come up with an excuse for why he'd been there at the exact time she'd needed him most.

That notion resurrected the wanting to believe that this awareness she felt may not be as one-sided as she'd thought. She had only to think back to his firmly spoken, *You'll be more comfortable when we get you resettled at the Hunts',* to get things back in perspective. He wanted her gone. And who could blame him.

"I'd stopped by to see you before," he added when she didn't press him for more.

"You had?" This, now this, was interesting. Jamie Morris, the young woman on the plane who was to have been Albert Payune's mail order bride, had visited her several times. Another one of Matt's friends, a fellow Cattleman's Club member, Aaron Black and Pamela Miles—now Pamela Black—and the Hunts had stopped in as well. She'd never known if she had been disappointed or profoundly relieved each time her door had swung open and it hadn't been Matthew on the other side.

"You were either sleeping or having therapy," he explained. "Or you'd developed an infection and they weren't allowing visitors."

"I'm sorry I missed you." She watched as he leaned forward in his chair, slowly rolling his empty glass between his big capable hands, hands that had held her on a dance floor and carried her on an escape route. Strong hands. Sure hands, tanned and lean. She thought of her left hand, no longer strong, no longer sure, and tucked it deeper into the folds of her robe.

When she looked up, he was watching her. She felt herself flush. She was sure he was about to say something about her hand, but instead, he set the empty glass on a side table then lifted a hand to her nightgown and robe. "The gown. The fit is okay?"

She was twenty-seven years old, the subject of countless feet of news footage, lived on constant public display and yet she felt another rush of heat rise to color her cheeks. How civilized they were. And how intimate as she sat here in a bedroom in his house in a pale blue gown and matching robe that covered her from neck to toe, and he asked about the fit.

"It fits just fine. Lois said it belongs to one of your sisters?"

"Becca. She keeps a room full of clothes here. Until Greg sends one of his hands over with your luggage tomorrow, feel free to use whatever you need."

"And your sister won't mind?"

"No. She won't mind. Becca is completely and irrevocably in love with her husband and her life in California.

If she makes it home more than twice a year, we're always surprised, but she leaves some of her things here so she doesn't have to drag them back and forth. Kay on the other hand does a lot of traveling with her career. We see her more often.''

He stopped abruptly then shook his head as if he'd just come to a realization. ''I'm so sorry, Helena. You have to be exhausted. I'm keeping you up when you need to sleep.''

''I've enjoyed this. Your company. The wine. It was perfect. Thank you. And thank you for helping me today. I don't know how I can ever repay you.''

His eyes met hers and across the few feet separating them, she thought she saw a suggestion there. The suggestion of a mutually satisfying form of repayment that altered her heartbeat and warmed her skin.

She'd been right. There was nothing uncomplicated about this man. In fact, a man who could touch a woman with his eyes and make her feel the pull as if he had physically enticed her toward him must be very complex.

Abruptly, he looked away, and just that easily, reminded her that it was only her fantasy that kept interrupting reality. The reality was, her accident had changed who and what she was—and what she could be to a man like him.

During the silence that harbored that painful truth, he rose and walked to the door. ''Rest well.'' He turned, pausing with his hand on the knob. ''I'll be just down the hall. Use the intercom if you need anything.''

Helena forced a smile. Well, that was it, wasn't it? He was leaving. Her heart had not yet recovered and he was leaving. Tomorrow or the next day, she'd be gone from High Stakes and in all likelihood never see Matthew Walker again.

It wasn't enough, she realized with no small sense of

panic. She wanted more. The part of her that was used to years of getting more overrode those new and unfamiliar insecurities that had yet to become cemented in her psyche.

If this brief time was all she could have of him—a fleeting moment, a soft smile—then she wanted one last contact. Despite the threat of rejection, it came as no small revelation that she wanted to test this attraction she felt. To see if, perhaps, she hadn't merely imagined a return spark.

She'd been a risk taker her entire life. Wasn't Matthew Walker worth another risk? She'd found out during the past two months that she could live with many things she'd never thought possible. She could live with the outcome if he rejected her—but she didn't think she could live with the knowledge that she'd been too much of a coward to even try.

"Matthew."

He turned.

And her heart stalled.

"I...I hate to ask, but I'm afraid I haven't been completely honest. I've over-extended a bit. Would you... could you..." She stopped, swallowed, and raised her eyes slowly to his. "I'm not sure I can make it to the bed on my own power."

It was a lie. Boldface and brazen. Her ankle hurt, yes. The ten steps to the bed would be difficult, but not impossible. What seemed impossible, suddenly, was letting him leave without touching her again.

He was at her side in two long strides, scooping her up as if she was made of spun glass and lifting her effortlessly into his arms.

"Why didn't you say something earlier?"

His breath was warm and wine-scented as it whispered richly across her cheek. She looped her left arm around his neck; her right hand rested naturally on his chest, just below his collarbone. Beneath her open palm, his heart beat steady and strong. His body heat leached through his clothes and her gown like a summer sun, nigh noon.

She lifted her face to his…to say something…to tell him something…something inane and chatty that would diffuse a tension that was suddenly so thick with awareness that she could hardly draw a breath—but she got caught in the wonder of his eyes instead. They were dark and restless now, as dark as emeralds, as restless as a midnight sea.

Her breath caught as his gaze, deeply intense, carnally sensual, dropped to her mouth. And lingered.

With a slow sweep of his dark lashes, he met her eyes again. For the longest, headiest moment, she thought he was going to kiss her. And she knew, without ever knowing the touch of his lips to hers that they would be firm and gentle, hot and hungry.

She lowered her lashes in anticipation, her heart wildly beating as his warm breath fanned her temple then pressed a very tender, very chaste kiss there. Then he lowered her carefully to the floor.

Even knowing her eyes were swimming with disappointment, she raised her gaze to his.

His touch was gentle as he brushed a fall of hair behind her ear. He swallowed thickly, his caress lingering in her hair as he bent to touch his lips to her brow in a kiss so gentle it made her ache. So brief, it made her yearn.

"Good night, Helena," he murmured hoarsely. Then he turned and walked out the door.

And left her there.

Alone.

With her heartbeat raging.

Her breath short and shallow.

And her mind drawing conclusions that were brutally and painfully honest.

She'd taken the risk and she'd lost.

His abrupt departure said it all. Matthew Walker wasn't a man who would walk away from what he wanted. Which meant only one thing. He didn't want her.

It hadn't been desire she'd seen in his eyes. It had been compassion. And the pain that knowledge fostered was more crippling than any injury she had yet endured.

Five

"Well, you're in a fine mood now, ain't ya?"

Matt tugged his left glove off with his teeth, then very systematically, removed the right, one finger at a time. He stuffed both in his hip pocket with a distracted glance at Frank, who was looking peeved, his bushy brows pinched with curiosity. "Let's just get this done, okay?"

Frank's wizened old face scrunched into a shrewd squint beneath his dusty brown Resistol. "That fancy lady you brought home yesterday responsible for that burr you got tucked under your saddle, boy?"

Matt filled his lungs with crisp March morning air and squatted down to grab the loose bottom board on the corral fence. Frank and Lois were the only two people in this world—short of his father—who he'd let get by with calling him boy, in that tone, in that way.

The fact that Frank was right, however, didn't make it

any easier to swallow. That "fancy lady" had everything to do with his foul mood.

"Hand me that sack of nails, would you?"

Frank let go a snort of disgust and tossed the sack at Matt's feet. It landed with a puff of Texas dust.

"Hokay," Frank grumbled. "If that's the way you wanna play it. Don't talk about it."

"I don't intend to." Matt snagged a galvanized nail, hammered the tenpenny home.

"Just let it fester. Let it—"

"Frank." He looked up, met the older man's eyes with a patient but pointed glare. "Let it go, okay?"

Frank tugged off his hat, raked his fingers through his thinning silver hair and resettled it on his head. "Fine. I got fence to check." Then, short of kicking a clod, he ambled off to the barn with his bowlegged gait to saddle up old Bill.

Matt almost stopped him, but, in the end, he went back to work on the broken corral fence. This wasn't a morning for one of Frank's well-intended lectures. This was a morning he needed to be alone.

That's why he'd been out here since sunup driving his men crazy and pushing Frank away. While he spent his fair share of time with the horses, he usually didn't interfere with the day-to-day operations of the ranch. Vince, his ranch manager, had already had a man on the repairs when Matt had intervened and taken over the chore. He'd needed some distance. He'd needed some time.

He'd needed to hit something.

The hammer in his hand was going to take care of that need. He wasn't sure about the rest of it. He was sure of only one thing. He'd made a mistake going to see Helena last night.

What the hell had he been thinking? He should have left

well enough alone, but no, he'd come up with a dozen excuses to justify a visit to her room. He'd been concerned about how she had settled in; he'd needed to play the host; he'd wanted to make sure she wasn't in pain or intimidated by Lois.

He'd needed to see her.

That, unfortunately, had been the bottom line.

Well, he'd drawn a new line in the cold clear light of morning. One he didn't intend to cross. As of today, Helena Reichard's bedroom was as off-limits as a nuclear test site. He could get too damn used to the feel of her in his arms. Too caught up in the fantasy of seeing her in his bed. Naked. Beneath him.

Disgusted with himself, he slammed another nail home. "You're an insensitive, testosterone-driven jerk, Walker, if the best you can do by her is feed your fantasies by thinking of ways to get her between the sheets."

Man, the last time he'd been this hot for a woman had been in high school. Didn't that just make him special.

After testing the repair, Matt rose to his feet and found himself chewing on memories of his marriage to Jena—a part of his past that should be reminder enough of why Helena Reichard wasn't the woman for him.

He propped his arms over the top rail, looked out over the dry lot where the yearlings frisked in the morning sun. This was his life. This was what he wanted for a life.

He didn't need to be out here working alongside his men. He didn't need to work a damn day for the rest of his life if he didn't want to. Between the oil leases, his stock investments and the portfolio of profitable businesses he'd bankrolled over the years, he'd increased the Walker coffers tenfold since he'd taken over from his father.

Despite his fortune, he was a simple man. He enjoyed simple pleasures. He liked the land, his horses and his association with the Cattleman's Club. A woman like Helena was a complication he couldn't afford.

Expression grim, he snagged his tools and headed for the tack house. Aside from his own reasons for keeping his distance, there were other things to consider besides his libido. Her, for instance.

She was still healing. Physically and emotionally, if his read on her was accurate. It had to be hell for her. Dealing with the pain. With the scarring. With physical limitations that might very well curtail, long-term, her prominent position in the international spotlight.

Though she would never admit to it, she was vulnerable right now. In so many ways. Beneath the confident, flirtatious exterior, the woman he'd whisked around the dance floor was a woman who, if caught unawares, was now quietly reflective. Oh, she said all the right things, but it was apparent that she had to work to keep a smile in place, dig deep for those snappy comebacks. No doubt her sense of desirability was also threatened.

If she only knew. If only he could tell her without making matters worse.

As bushed as he'd been, he'd lain awake half the night wanting her. Thinking about that kiss he'd almost stolen. Wishing he hadn't backed away at the last minute. Wanting to show her just how desirable she was.

If he followed through on that wish, he wouldn't exactly be playing to her needs, though, would he? He'd be building on his. That's why he'd backed away. Hell. Whether she was willing to admit it or not, she was as defenseless as an orphan in the wild.

With her startlingly blue eyes, creamy white skin and silken fall of long blond hair, she looked about as fragile as a rose under the Texas sun. The last thing she needed was him taking advantage of her and leading her headlong into a love affair. And that's all it could ever be between them. A sweet, hot affair.

But man, would it be sweet.

And damn, would it be hot.

And then, it would be over.

He tossed the tool bucket onto the workbench.

No. She didn't need an affair and neither did he. And he definitely wasn't looking for a relationship—even if he were, it wouldn't be with a woman like her. A woman who shone brightest in the limelight and fed off the sparks of her own fire. He'd been down that road with Jena and he wasn't about to run that route again.

Since the divorce seven years ago, he'd had his share of civilized, and by mutual agreement, temporary relationships. By choice, it had been a while since he'd been involved with anyone. A long while, he realized when he thought about it. Maybe that explained this physical tug he felt toward Helena. It had been a long dry spell.

Yeah. And maybe Milo Yungst and Garth Johannes, those two goons who were supposedly representatives of the Asterland government, were really here checking on the reason for the plane crash.

He couldn't shake his bad feelings about them. Couldn't throw the notion that there was more to them then met the eye—and none of it good.

The unknown threat against Helena alone ought to be enough to prompt him to get his head out of his pants and remember why she was here in the first place. She needed his protection, and until he had her firmly entrenched at the Hunts'—by tomorrow, he hoped—that's the only role he had to play in her life. Once she was with Greg and Anna, then distance, at least, would take care of the immediate temptation of having her so near.

In the meantime, he was acting like a jerk. Just because

he was having a problem didn't mean he didn't have some obligations. She was his guest. And he was proving to be a sorry excuse for a host.

He glanced out the tack-room window, looked toward the house then checked his watch. It was after 8:00 a.m. Surely she was awake by now. Hard telling how she and Lois were managing. If he were any kind of a man—any kind of a decent man—he'd make sure she wasn't wanting for anything.

With a deep breath, he looked at the sky then set his mind to the task. He headed for the house. He could do this. He could be kind and considerate, and he could make sure she was comfortable. And he could keep his hands to himself in the process.

But then he walked into the kitchen. He saw her sitting at the breakfast nook. She was glassy-eyed, her smile braced up by breeding and manners as Lois served her tea and toast and more chatter than any mortal should be asked to endure. She looked dazed and a little frantic and a lot in need of rescuing.

When she spotted him, the relief in her eyes and the look she shot over Lois's head was desperate and pleading. "Help me," it said. "I'm in over my head here, but I don't want to hurt her feelings."

In a heartbeat, the part of him that had shored up enough resistance to head-butt a tank folded like a pup tent in a stout wind. And right on cue, the white knight he'd never realized was such a part of him charged in to save the day—again.

"All set?" Matt asked as he rounded the golf cart and slipped behind the wheel.

Helena sat in the passenger seat, looking elegant and

regal and delighted with the workings of the cherry-red electric cart.

"What ingenious transportation."

"I bought this for Lois a few years ago. Saves her a lot of steps from their house to the main house. And the bright color has probably saved a lot of lives," he added with a grin. "You can't miss her coming at you. Frank calls it her little red mayhem mobile. The woman is hell on wheels."

He slipped his foot from the brake to the accelerator and was about to pull away when she touched a hand to his arm. Now that the glazed look of panic Lois had put in her eyes had faded, he realized that she looked more rested today. The March wind lifted her long blond hair away from her face and added a heart-melting trace of pink to her cheeks.

Along with news that the press was still camped out near Casa Royale, one of Greg's hands had delivered her luggage bright and early this morning. Her charcoal turtle-neck sweater looked as soft as her skin and as warm as her eyes. Her slacks were black, the Italian leather slouch boot on her left foot sophisticated and tailored. Beneath her removable cast, the toes of her left foot were covered with a warm black stocking.

"Thank you for this. It's lovely to get out in the fresh air."

"Getting a little stifling in the house, was it?"

"Oh, I hope I didn't give the wrong impression. Lois is wonderful. I don't want you to think—"

"You don't want me to think that you felt cornered?" he interrupted, feeling the need to tease that concern off her face. "Maybe a little caged in? How about smothered with kindness and questions and if I hadn't walked into the kitchen when I had and gotten you out of there that

you'd have curled into a fetal position and started screaming at the top of your lungs?''

Her blue eyes sparkled as she tried, unsuccessfully, to
hide a smile of relief.

He angled her a crooked grin. ''Well, don't worry about
it. Because I didn't think that at all.''

She actually laughed then. The sound of it sang on the
light breeze, mellow and sweet and in complete harmony
with the sun-drenched morning. Even more pleasing was
the spontaneity that had prompted her laughter. Not since
the night he'd met her had he seen that much life, witnessed that much unguarded delight dance in her eyes. He
liked it. He liked her.

''She's just so…so much,'' she finally said, the warmth
of her laughter still singing in her voice. ''She's truly de-
lightful. And a kinder person I've yet to meet. But, oh,
that energy. I don't believe I've ever heard anyone talk
that long with that much exuberance and animation.''

''What she is, is exhausting,'' he said with a fondness
he couldn't curb. ''Just make sure I don't pick up where
she left off and tire you out too much. You get tired or
cold, you let me know, okay, and we'll head back to the
house.''

Her smile was as soft as summer when she nodded and
diverted her attention to the sites around her as he headed
out of the house yard at a slow, easy speed. The expression
on her face made her look young and carefree and, for the
first time since he'd brought her to High Stakes, relaxed.
It also relayed a confidence in him that he wasn't sure he
deserved.

Her faith in him reminded him that whatever it was that
was going on between them wasn't about him. It was about
her. It was about how badly she needed to distance herself
from her limitations and embrace the fact that life was still

good. That, more than she needed him as a prospective lover, she needed him as a friend. Someone to show her the dawn when she had been living for two months near the dark.

Well, that was it then, wasn't it? He glanced thoughtfully at her profile then back to the path. For as long as she was here, he would do everything in his power to be her friend. For a fact, he figured she was probably in need of one.

With that firmly in mind, he set out to be just that. A friend. Nothing more.

With cordial hospitality, he pointed out a compact dwelling bordered by a colorful cactus garden.

"We've offered to build Lois and Frank a new house several times," he said as he slowed to a stop in front of the neatly kept grounds of an adobe ranch house, "but just like retiring, they won't hear of it. Lois just says, 'I took and raised my girls here, and when they think of coming home, it's to this house. That's enough to keep me here and them coming back.'"

When she asked, he told her about Lois's two daughters who both lived in Galveston with their families and came back to see their folks for all major holidays and a few visits in between.

"Vince and Amy live here," he said as they approached a smaller version of his own house. "Vince is my ranch manager—you'll meet him later. He's amazing with the horses and great with the men. Amy is the pretty young woman you met this morning at the main house. Lois would never admit it—and God forbid I ever point it out— but she's getting a little old to be doing much housework. Amy very quietly makes sure what needs to be done gets done. Except in the kitchen. It'll take a war to get Lois out of there."

"I'd say you can be very thankful for that. The dinner she prepared last evening was wonderful."

He angled her a look, grinned. "So, you like Tex-Mex, do you?"

"I'd like anything after two months of hospital food, but actually, yes. If it's all like what Lois prepares, I do like it. It's very…lively."

"Lively. Now there's a word. Just wait until you taste her chili."

They exchanged a look then that echoed each other's thoughts. Chances were Helena wouldn't be around High Stakes long enough to sample Lois's chili or any number of her special dishes.

He thought her smile was a little wistful when she looked toward the horizon. Or maybe he was reading in his own feelings. In a couple of days she'd be gone and that would be the end of that. In silence, he turned toward the barns, telling himself it would be for the best.

The wind had come up by midmorning, as Matt had told Helena it so often did. She hadn't wanted to admit it— she'd been so taken with this intimate look at High Stakes, especially Matt's new crop of colts and fillies in the foaling barn—but she was exhausted. Evidently, it had shown, because Matthew had insisted on taking her back to the house a little before noon.

They'd shared a quiet lunch on the veranda overlooking the gardens and the indoor pool. He was very careful to keep the conversation neutral and benign as he told her about his cutting horses, about his breeding program, the intricacies of the training, the rewards of competition.

She could have protested a little more, she supposed, when he'd insisted on carrying her up the stairs to her room afterwards. She could have, but he seemed so intent on playing the perfect host, she let it go. And when he'd left her by the bed with little more than a tip of his hat— fawn-colored today—and a, "Rest. I'll see you at dinner," she let that go, too.

He was, after all, merely fulfilling an obligation. He'd been clever, amusing, cordial, polite, informative—and distant. So distant and detached, that she'd felt the slightest bit of a chill despite the warm March sun.

His arms hadn't been cold. Cradled against him, she'd felt warmth and strength and a sense of closeness that undercut the emotional distance he'd placed between them all morning.

Still, she understood what he was doing. Just as she understood the reason he hadn't kissed her last night when he'd left her. He was, as kindly as possible, making it clear that there was nothing but circumstance that had drawn them together. It was just as well then, that there was probably nothing more than a scant twenty-four hours until those same circumstances would draw them apart.

Determined not to open herself up for another rejection, she decided to accept his ground rules. There would be no romance with Matthew Walker. And how could she blame him? It was a small step to cement truth in reality when she took a long, thorough look at herself in the full-length mirror after her bath.

The mirror that had always been kind to her was now brutally and painfully cruel. Even if Matthew had encouraged her, she understood that it would be a long time before she would be strong enough or brave enough to invite a man to her bed. It would take more trust than she was capable of garnering to believe that any man could overlook her scars and accept her as she was. Accept *who* she was—whoever that was, she thought grimly and limped to the bed.

Only because she was physically exhausted did she sleep. When she awoke, she dressed in soft champagne-colored silk that covered her arms and legs—and fought tears of frustration over the difficulty of a once simple and uneventful task.

With quiet dignity, she brushed her hair and applied a light touch of makeup. Then she made herself a promise.

"I will stop thinking about Matthew Walker as anything but what he is. A nice man who is being gracious and hospitable and who is merely fulfilling a commitment his good manners will not allow him to walk away from."

With that, she slipped into her boot cast and a soft ballerina flat and limped slowly from the room.

She ignored the pain. To acknowledge it meant giving in to it and she wanted very badly to be finished with defeat. She wanted very badly for her injuries to stop ruling her life. And she wanted, very badly, to find the strength to make that happen.

When Helena found Matthew in the dining room, she ignored the erratic little scramble her heartbeat insisted on performing every time she saw him.

A bottle of wine in his hand, he looked up from a bleached pine sideboard, surprise in his eyes. "I was about to come for you."

"Oh, I know what you were about to do." She eased down onto the chair he pulled out for her and willed her heart to settle. "You were about to carry me down the stairs again when I can manage perfectly under my own steam."

"You're little more than a day out of the hospital," he insisted. "There's no point in pushing too hard."

"There's every point. I've put my life on hold long enough."

He searched her face as he uncorked a bottle of merlot.

"I'm doing fine, Matthew. Really. If I need your assistance, I promise, I'll ask for it."

Not looking completely satisfied, he conceded with a nod anyway, perceptive enough to realize that she wanted the subject closed. "Fair enough."

He showed her the bottle.

"Thank you, yes." She smiled and tried not to notice the ultra-masculine appeal of his hands, tanned, work-roughened, lightly dusted with short, sun-bleached hair.

That her own hand wasn't noticeably shaking when she lifted the glass to her lips came as both surprise and relief. "This is wonderful. Lois knows her wines."

He grinned and, despite her resolve not to let it, her tummy did that little somersault it was wont to do just at the look of him.

"Actually," he said, oblivious to her reaction, "Lois is a teetotaler from way back. You can blame me if it doesn't suit."

She lifted a brow, this new facet of Matthew reconfirming that the man was definitely more complicated than he let on. "Are you a connoisseur, then?"

"Hardly. I invested in a little vineyard in southern California several years ago. I like to sample the results."

"Ah. A man of many interests."

He tilted his head, shrugged. "A businessman."

"Who prefers the desert to the boardroom," she said with open speculation. "How intriguing."

"What can I say? I'm a true son of the desert."

"A child of the West," she concluded and waited for his reaction.

"I guess you could say it's in the blood," he admitted and pulling out a chair, sat at the table, at cross-corners to her.

The unplanned intimacy—just the two of them sitting together at his table, flirting over wine—reminded her, with a sharp little twist to her heart, of how much she would have liked to have been a long-term part of this lovely picture that was High Stakes and Matthew Walker.

"High Stakes," she murmured, looking out the arched windows to the grounds beyond in an attempt to distance herself from the moment. "It's an interesting name. Something tells me there's also an interesting story behind it."

"There's always an interesting story in Texas."

When he smiled, she told herself she wasn't lost. She was merely intrigued and that the thready thrum of her pulse was caused by the wine, not his nearness. She lifted her glass, and when his eyes met and held hers above the rim, she scrambled to believe it was just coincidence, that he hadn't really been as intent on her as she had been on him. "You *are* going to tell me the story, aren't you?"

After a long moment, he drank, then started talking.

"The long and the short of it is that my great-great-great-grandfather, Clint Walker, loved nothing better than a high stakes game of poker. Evidently, he was good at it because, among other things, he won this land—all twenty thousand acres—in one dramatic hand of five-card stud. That was back before Texas had even applied for statehood. High Stakes has been Walker land ever since."

"High stakes, indeed," she said, as delighted with the romance of the story as she was taken with the man telling it.

He leaned forward, elbows propped on the table, his glass gripped loosely in his hand. "Not exactly the most noble method of starting a family dynasty."

The slightest trace of guilt in his expression made her smile. "Oh my, no. European methods are definitely more respectable. My ancestors merely pillaged and plundered their way to prosperity.''

He chuckled softly.

She watched him in momentary silence before her curiosity got the best of her. "So, you've no dramatic call to destiny that compels you, no burning desire that drives you to be anywhere else but here?''

He lifted a shoulder. "That pretty well sums it up. My father retired a few years ago and he and Mother resettled on the Gulf. Becca and Kay both migrated to the west coast without a backward glance. Except for a hitch in the marines—a Walker tradition that began with my great-grandfather Cal—and five years at Texas State, High Stakes has pretty much been my life.''

Clearly, Matt was a man of the land, his own man, and he saw no reason to disrupt or alter his life. And then there was the undeniable draw of High Stakes and Texas.

"I think I can understand why," she said reflectively. "It's beautiful here. I could get used to it. The quiet. The solitude.''

A tight smile played around his mouth. "No disrespect, but I find that a little hard to believe.''

She lifted a brow, a little sorry for her unplanned confession, a lot curious about the trace of bitterness in his voice. "Why? Because I was born to the titled European aristocracy? Because what you know of me is most likely a media-fabricated image?''

He regarded her a bit sadly, she thought. "Because you are a beautiful woman and my experience with beautiful women is that they prefer civilization and cities and all the varied and festive accoutrements that go with them to solitude and breathtaking sunsets.''

She leaned back in her chair, regarded him thoughtfully and not for the first time wondered about the women in his life. Had there actually been a woman foolish enough to break his heart?

"Well," she said, instead of asking what she really wanted to ask, "it's difficult to argue with a cynic, I suppose, isn't it?"

He leaned back too, hooking an arm over the chair's ladder-back. He looked not at her, but at the sparkling glass of wine he held in his hand. "Were we arguing?"

"Yes," she said after a long, contemplative moment. "I think perhaps we were."

The question was, why? She'd dismissed his reference to her being a beautiful woman out of hand. Compliments, true or false, came to him as naturally as breathing and she could not easily forget that she was forever altered physically. What intrigued her was this new, darker facet to his personality. It didn't fit with what she knew of him. Unfortunately, neither did it detract from his appeal. And it didn't stop her from wanting to know more.

"Are you truly a cynic, Matthew?"

He took his time responding, as if he were trying to decide how much of himself he wanted to reveal to her. When he finally spoke, she was disappointed that he chose to evade the question.

"What I am is hungry. It tends to make me a little cranky. I apologize," he said with a finality that told her the subject was closed.

She really had little choice. "Accepted," she said after a brief moment.

"Shall we?" He lifted a silver lid from the chafing dish centered on the table.

Two smiles, polite and guarded, met across the polished pine. "By all means."

Quite obviously, the subject of what made Matthew Walker tick was off-limits. It was just as well, she decided

as they enjoyed another of Lois's delicious meals and re-
treated into a conversation about horses that was familiar
to both of them—and entirely safe. Safe, because he did
not have to reveal anything of himself to her. Safe, because
she did not have to reveal anything of herself to him.

Safe, because, if ever there had been a man who could
persuade her to relinquish her secrets, her insecurities, it
was this man—and this man couldn't have made it clearer
that he did not want to know.

That knowledge didn't hurt her. As she lay in bed later
that night, listening to the midnight sounds, staring into
the moon-drenched night, the tear that trickled slowly
down her temple and into her hair had nothing to do with
wishing he had cared for her enough to ask. It had nothing
to do with knowing that if he had, she might have told
him anything. Anything. And with the telling, she might
have given him her heart.

"You're not serious?" Sitting in the library, Matt
rocked back in the leather desk chair. He dragged a hand
through his hair as he fought to accept Greg Hunt's news.

"'Fraid so. We're flying out this morning. Damned in-
convenient sometimes, being married to a woman who has
a country to run." The pride and affection in Greg's voice
undercut the staged complaint of his words. "Something
about a problem in the security system at the casino. Sorry,
Matt. Look, I've got to run. We're cutting it close as it is.
Helena will be fine with you, right?"

Matt mumbled the obligatory, "Right. Don't worry
about it. You need to take care of your own," and hung
up.

This was not good.

This was not good at all.

He thought back to last night. To the quiet dinner he

had shared with Helena. He'd liked seeing her at his table.
He'd liked too much the intelligence of her conversation.
And he'd had to guard himself too carefully or he would
have been spilling his guts about his marriage to Jena,
about this growing attraction he felt for her. He'd have
been asking her to confide in him about how she felt about
herself, about what hurt her, about that pride that made her
so damn strong.

She was too irresistible. She was too vulnerable. She
was too everything, and he'd known by the end of the
evening that despite his resolve to send her to the Hunts',
he was going to have a hard time letting her go anywhere.

And now, it appeared that she would be staying.

Surely there were other options? He couldn't ask Aaron
and Pamela. They were barely back from their honeymoon.
Sheikh Ben Rassad had his hands full watching out for
Jamie Morris who had been on the plane with Helena and
may also be in danger. Besides, as much as he liked and
trusted the handsome sheikh who was his neighbor and
friend, the thought of turning Helena over to all that mysterious middle-eastern charm didn't set well. There was
Justin, but he was little more than a newlywed himself. He
and Winona were completely mired in each other and the
baby they were in the process of adopting.

That left Dakota Lewis, the last of the five club members
trying to solve the puzzle surrounding the missing diamond
and Riley's death. Dakota was more than capable of protecting Helena. But, like Ben, he was another one of those
darkly good-looking men. As far as Matt was concerned,
that was enough of a reason to dismiss him out of hand,
even though it was obvious to everyone but Dakota that
he still carried a torch for his estranged wife.

Refusing to dwell on why he didn't see either Dakota
or Ben as an option, he picked up the phone and dialed

Aaron's number. The obvious solution was to get this thing wrapped up so Helena was no longer at risk. Until they did, it looked like she would be remaining at High Stakes, and he wasn't going to be able to get on with his life—for that matter, neither was she.

"Black residence."

"Pamela. It's Matt."

"Matt! How are you?"

He smiled at the warmth in her voice. "The question is how are you? Never mind. I think I've got that one figured out by the sound of your voice. I take it married life is agreeing with you."

"Married life is fabulous."

"I'm glad. And I'm apologizing in advance for calling, but I need to talk to Aaron."

"Not a problem. He's right here."

A few seconds later, Aaron came on the line. "Hey, Matt. What's up?"

"Two things. One, the five of us need to meet."

"I've been thinking the same thing."

"Two, Helena Reichard was released from the hospital the day before yesterday."

"So I heard. The big question buzzing around town is where did she go? She seems to have disappeared into thin air. The press are going crazy trying to bring her to ground."

Briefly, Matt explained that Helena was with him at High Stakes and how she ended up there.

"Here's the problem—she has a string of medical appointments this afternoon, so I've got to get her into town. Greg and Anna were going to help but Anna's been called back to Obersbourg. I don't want the press or anyone but the five of us knowing where she is, so I can't afford to have her seen in any of my vehicles or they'll make the connection."

"Say no more. Tell me what time you need us to show up at High Stakes, and Pamela and I will be there."

He'd known he could count on Aaron. "Thanks, man. In the meantime, I'll see what I can do about gathering the rest of the troops. If Pamela can stay with Helena during her clinic visits, the five of us can get together at the club for an hour or so."

And then maybe, just maybe, Matt thought, as he disconnected, they could make some forward progress.

Matt found Helena out on the terrace half an hour later. He stood for a moment and simply watched her. The sunlight danced across the golden highlights of her hair as a soft breeze lifted it away from her face and stirred the leaves of an overhanging crape myrtle.

It was as difficult to read her reaction when he broke the news about Greg and Anna's unplanned trip to Obersbourg as it was to control his urge to brush a silken strand away from her face and tuck it behind her ear.

He knew why he was suddenly quiet. He wasn't sure why she was, as she looked, with what seemed like longing, over the gardens and the endless desert plains beyond.

When she finally met his eyes, they were blank of emotion, utterly unreadable. "If I could just use your phone, I can make arrangements with the Royalton Hotel. I'm sure they'll send a car for me."

If he were being honest, he might admit—at least to himself—that he'd been hoping for a little twinge of regret on her part. He wasn't sure how he felt when she didn't show any. Relief is what he should have felt. And maybe a sense of satisfaction that he'd been right about her. That she was only being polite when she'd insisted she was taken with High Stakes. That he'd been right to believe that titled ladies and desert plains mixed about as well as chili powder and crème brûlée.

He didn't much feel like smiling over the fact that she seemed to find it so easy to leave, but he did anyway. For his sake, if not for hers. And then he told himself that the reason he was suddenly so determined that she stay when an hour ago he'd been desperate to get her out of his hair was that her life might still be in danger. Of course, she didn't know that. She wasn't going to know it as long as it was within his power to keep it from her.

The danger, he finally admitted, was only part of it. She was facing an entirely different threat here at High Stakes, but since the only thing he had to protect her from was himself, he figured he had an edge on keeping her out of that particular line of fire.

"There's no need for you to move to the hotel," he said casually and tried to read the expression in the eyes that lifted with quiet expectancy to his. "You're welcome at High Stakes for as long as you need to stay."

It might have been hope that flickered in those brilliant blue depths. It might have been relief. And it might have been a lot of wishful thinking on his part when her softly murmured, "I don't wish to impose on you, Matthew," rode on the stillness of the morning.

"Impose? I promise you'll be doing me a favor. The truth is, I'm in a little hot water with Lois over the fact that you were going to be moving to the Hunts'. She says you've created the most excitement around Royal since that Hunt boy married the princess."

It wasn't a lie exactly. He'd just embellished the truth a bit.

"So help me out here, okay?" he coaxed when her lips curved into a slow and utterly enchanting smile. "Say you'll stay. Make me the good guy—at least in Lois's eyes.''

She'd looked away from him then, a smile still tilting her lips as she squinted, quite beautifully, against the sun. ''Well, what with you wearing that nice white hat today, I suppose that's the only role you could play, isn't it?''

He didn't know whether to laugh or swear at the relief her concession created. And he didn't know if she should be running instead of smiling. He might be wearing his white hat, but if she knew what he thought about at night, if she knew how he ached to tumble her across his bed, she'd have him pegged for the bad guy in a black hat in a heartbeat.

Six

An hour later, the four of them, Pamela and Aaron, Matt and Helena, were on the road to town. The trip into Royal, for all the catastrophic potential, went as smoothly as silk. Since the press was still halfway convinced that Helena was with the Hunts, they hadn't been looking for her in Aaron's big black luxury car. With Pamela at her side for support, Helena was now safely tucked away at the clinic for a series of exams and X rays. After that she'd have physical therapy that would keep her there for the better part of two hours.

Matt checked his watch as Aaron drove down the main street toward the Cattleman's Club, which was located on the outskirts of town.

"We've got a few minutes. Let's stop at the diner—see if we can pick up on any chatter about Helena or the plane crash."

Aaron shrugged. "Worth a try. Besides, it's been a long

time since I've had one of Manny Hernandez's pecan rolls.''

"Well, there is that," Matt said with a grin as Aaron pulled the black sedan into a parking place outside the Royal Diner.

Half an hour later, they walked into the ultra-masculine, ultra-luxurious interior of the Texas Cattleman's Club. Matt looked around the room and returned nodding hellos to the four men seated at a round table in the corner of the room. Hank Langley, the great-grandson of Tex Langley, the club's founder, Forrest Cunningham, Sterling Churchill, and Greg Hunt's brother, Blake, returned to a good-natured, but heated, card game.

When Matt spotted Dakota Lewis at the far end of the polished oak bar, he and Aaron walked toward him.

Dakota jerked his head toward an intricately carved walnut door at the end of the hall after the three men exchanged handshakes. "Ben and Justin are already in the back room."

Justin was seated at the central table. He looked up from his coffee when the three of them entered the ornately appointed private meeting room. "Afternoon, gentlemen."

Matt nodded to Justin and clasped a hand to Sheikh Ben Rassad's shoulder in greeting then reached for a bone-china cup with the club's crest embossed in gold. He drew coffee from the silver urn that was set in the middle of the table, took a sip.

"Now this," he said pointedly to Justin, "is coffee."

Justin smirked. "You're a lightweight, Walker."

Taking no offense at Justin's grinning jab, Matt scanned the faces around the room. "Let's get down to business, shall we?"

Dakota, standing with an elbow propped on the marble

mantel, made a sound of disbelief. "What? No horse talk?"

Matt exchanged a smile with Ben, who Matt had come to know and like since he'd bought an adjacent ranch and joined the club. "Maybe later. Anybody got anything for show-and-tell today?"

"Suppose you start with Helena," Justin suggested. "How is she? More specifically, *where* is she?"

"She's one tough lady, that's how she is—or so she would have everyone think," Matt added and thought about the apprehension on her face when he'd left her at the clinic with Pamela. He hadn't wanted to leave her. Because he'd had no right to attach himself to those proprietary feelings, and because they weren't going to do him any good at this meeting, he shrugged them off.

"As to where is she, for the long haul, it looks like she'll be staying with me." He explained about the Hunts being called to Obersbourg and ignored the quick glances the other men exchanged. "For the short haul, she's at the clinic."

"Under guard?" Ben asked, his gray eyes smoky with concern beneath his kaffiyeh, the traditional headdress of his Amythra culture. His skin was as dark as a Texan's beneath his djellaba, the white robes that, like the kaffiyeh, he always wore in public.

Matt shook his head and tried not to feel too antsy about leaving Helena with Pamela, even for a short period of time.

"Are you not afraid someone will get to her?"

"You ever tried to get into a doctor's office without an appointment?" he said with a pointed, but grinning glance toward Justin.

Justin, conceding Matt's congenial but well-aimed slur

against the medical profession in general, merely shrugged. "The man's got a point."

"Okay," Aaron, ever the diplomat, interrupted, "let's get back on track. What's happening with the Blues Brothers, Dakota?"

The men all had their pet names for Garth Yungst and Milo Johannes—not all of them as kind as Aaron's.

While Matt, Aaron and Ben were assigned to safeguard the women, Dakota, retired air force, had been designated to keep an eye on the activities of the two investigators.

"They're way too shady for my taste." Dakota pulled out a chair. Propping a booted foot on the seat, he folded his forearms over his knee. "I've been running a background check but so far I've got zilch. Until something turns up, we've got nothing but what they say they are."

What they said they were was investigators sent by the Asterland government to explore every avenue concerning the jet's malfunction that had led to the crash. What all five men suspected, however, was that Yungst and Johannes were actually searching for the red diamond and the two jewels Justin had recovered at the crash site.

"Tell them about your conversation with Gretchen, Matt."

Matt quickly explained that when he and Aaron had stopped at the diner, he'd run into Gretchen Hansen, a nurse at Royal Memorial.

"She'd done a rotation in the burn unit when Helena was hospitalized and remembered seeing me in the halls. She evidently made an assumption that I knew where Helena was because she asked about her. Then she went on to tell me that Robert Klimt had come out of his coma a day or so ago but that he wasn't doing all that well."

"Klimt's out of the coma? That's news," Dakota said with a frown in Justin's direction.

"Hey—I've been busy," Justin said defensively. "I hadn't heard."

"Don't worry about it." Matt dismissed Justin's concern as inconsequential. "Besides, Gretchen had all the scoop—she's one very observant lady. She'd actually been in Klimt's hospital room when a news report aired about the crash and the continuing investigation. She said Klimt had gone as white as the bedsheets when he'd seen the report on TV. Then his blood pressure, which, according to Gretchen is still very unstable, went haywire."

"Could have been a post-traumatic reaction," Justin speculated. "Seeing the report would have brought it all back to him pretty graphically."

"You're right. It could have been," Aaron agreed. "It also could have meant that it made him nervous as hell. Like maybe he had something to hide?" He dangled the notion like bait.

"Klimt? I thought he was a member of King Bertram's cabinet," Ben said. "What would he have to be nervous about?"

"Nothing," Matt agreed, "if he was a *trusted* member of the Asterlander king's cabinet. If he wasn't…" He let the thought trail off.

"Then add to the mix the fact that Yungst and Johannes were pretty adamant about seeing him as soon as he recovered," Aaron pointed out.

"Yeah, but that would probably follow," Dakota reasoned aloud.

"Agreed, but would it also follow that they tossed around all kinds of threats about diplomatic immunity and strained political relations when Klimt's doctor wouldn't let them talk to him?" Matt looked from one grim face to the other. He could see their suspicions about Klimt taking root.

"Ramsey's his neurologist," Justin said, his brows drawn together in thought. "If he wouldn't let the boys see Klimt, it's because he considers his condition guarded. He must be too weak to be interviewed."

Matt nodded. "That would line up with what Gretchen said. At times, Klimt doesn't appear to know his own name, let alone remember any crash details."

"So," Dakota's foot hit the floor as he turned the chair around and braced his palms on its back. "Where does this leave us?"

Aaron, as ever thoughtful and pragmatic, restated the rumors he'd heard from fellow diplomats about the possibility of a revolution brewing in Asterland. As one, they all agreed that their growing suspicion that the jewels might have been stolen to fund it was starting to look like more than conjecture.

"You do realize," Ben said stoically, his eyes contemplative beneath his dark brows, "if that jet had not experienced a malfunction, we never would have connected Riley Monroe's murder and the theft of the jewels to the revolution."

"*If* there's a revolution. In any event, it's looking like a trip to Asterland is becoming more of a probability than a possibility," Justin added with a thoughtful look toward Dakota. "Has any one gotten hold of Kathy yet?"

Dakota's expression closed off at the mention of his estranged wife, but not before they'd all seen his initial reaction. That there was pain and unfinished business between Dakota and Kathy Lewis was apparent to every man in the room. That Kathy Lewis was the perfect foreign affairs specialist for the job since she was highly trusted by the Asterland royal court was the reason she would be called in on this mission. That it would be anyone but

Dakota who would accompany her was not up for discussion. He was the first choice. The only choice.

Aaron cleared his throat diplomatically. "We're working on it, but we've got a few fish to fry before it comes to firming up a trip to Asterland. We've got to find the missing diamond. And we've got to find Riley's murderer."

Matt nodded, the mention of the murder renewing his concern about Helena. "Until we do, Helena and Jamie are still at risk."

"And so, if the legend is accurate, is Royal's prosperity," Dakota added grimly, his face carefully blank of emotion.

"I've got to go see about Helena," Matt said, rising quickly from the table. All four men studied him with an open speculation he chose to ignore. "Keep your eyes open and your backs covered, gentlemen," he added, as they made promises to keep each other abreast of any new developments as they happened.

"So," Matt said as he followed Ben toward the door. "How's that little gelding working out for you?"

Matt had sold Ben the spirited sorrel along with two bay mares last fall when Ben had decided to add quarter horses to his Appaloosa program.

"I am starting to become a believer," Ben admitted.

"Never doubted for a minute that you would."

"I knew the two of you couldn't get out of here without talking a little horseflesh." This from Dakota who was already heading out the door and into the hall.

"What can I say?" Matt grinned. "We are, after all, in Texas."

As they entered the main salon, the men all sobered as, one by one, they looked toward the plaque above the door that only they knew temporarily hid the opal and the emerald, two of the Lone Star jewels.

Leadership. Justice. Peace. The three words carved into the plaque represented all that the club members held sacred. The stones represented all that made Royal prosper. And Matt was all too aware that until the diamond was reunited with the other two jewels, both Royal's future and Helena's remained at risk.

Aaron's black sedan was idling softly when Matt, with a disquietingly silent Helena at his side, slipped out the back door of the clinic. Aaron was already behind the wheel with Pamela in front beside him. Matt had just got Helena settled comfortably in the back seat when a brown four-door pulled into the parking lot, purposely blocking them in.

Aaron was out of the car in an instant, his expression grim as he moved to stand beside Matt. Both men braced for battle as Milo Yungst and Garth Johannes stepped out of the rental car and walked toward them.

"You're blocking our way, gentlemen," Matt said in a deceptively conversational tone as he squared off with the two men. Yungst, an Ichabod Crane look-alike, was tall and gangly with a head full of springy, wiry curls framing a long, angular face. In contrast, Johannes was as squat and stocky as a brick, his brown hair slicked back with about a gallon of cooking oil. Matt had disliked both of them the first time he'd seen them. Since then, nothing had happened to change his mind.

"Now, I'm willing to allow that it wasn't your intent," he said, his tone clearly conveying that he thought no such thing, "so what say you just get back in the car and we'll all be on our way?"

"Begging your pardon," this from Yungst, his protruding Adam's apple bobbing in his long, pencil-thin neck, "but we have business with Lady Reichard."

"Not today, you don't," Matt said stiffly, his eyes hard, his entire body tense. "Now move it, before I forget that my mother raised me to be a gentleman."

"We ask only a few moments of her time." Johannes, his beefy neck bulging over the top of his too-tight collar, his face gone red with burgeoning anger, attempted to look amicable. "We just need to hear from her, get her account of the emergency landing. To add her perspective to the others we have already interviewed."

"Interviewed?" Matt made no attempt to hide the venom in his voice. "Is that what you call your interrogations these days? Sorry, but, no dice. The lady is not getting grilled by you today."

"Grilled? Interrogation? Oh, but no. We merely wish to speak to her."

"Not today."

"But—"

"I said," Matt took a menacing step toward the duo, "this is not going to happen today."

Aaron moved up beside him, gripped Matt's arm as if holding him back, effectively playing good cop to Matt's bad cop. "This might be a good time to say good day, boys. He's starting to get upset. You really don't want to stick around to see that."

Yungst glanced at Johannes, hesitated for a moment, then grudgingly bowed his head. "Very well." He reached into his hip pocket, fished out his wallet and withdrew a card. He handed it to Matt. "My cell-phone number. Please ask the lady to contact me when she feels capable of answering a few questions."

Without looking at the card, Matt tucked it in his shirt

pocket. "Yeah, sure. I'll put that right at the top of my to-do list."

With a long, dark look, the two investigators from Asterland turned, got back in their car and drove away.

Matt grinned at Aaron as they watched them go. "How many Texans does it take to scare off a pug and a poodle?" he asked, recalling Justin's apt description of the pair.

"Two," Aaron answered, a smile hooking one corner of his mouth. "One with the disposition of a Doberman and one who looks like he's ready to yell sic 'em."

"What did they want?" Pamela asked when the men had settled in the car.

"They wanted to talk to Helena."

For the first time since Matt had gone in to find her waiting for him, Helena showed some animation—and maybe a little apprehension. "Me? Are they with the press?"

Matt watched her face. "No. They're from Asterland." When her brows furrowed, he explained. "They've been here for a little over a month now, investigating the circumstances surrounding the emergency landing."

She glanced from Matt to Aaron. "Investigating?"

"Sort of the Asterlander version of the FAA," Aaron supplied evasively.

"I don't understand. I thought the cause of the crash had been determined. That it was a system malfunction of some sort."

Matt met Aaron's gaze in the rearview mirror. A silent agreement passed between them to continue to keep Helena in the dark regarding their suspicions about the two men. "That's true," he hedged. "I guess they don't want to leave any stone unturned."

"Well, they give me the creeps," Pamela said with a shudder.

Helena looked thoughtful. "The one—the tall one. He seems familiar, somehow."

Matt was instantly alert. "Familiar?"

She shook her head, looked out the window. "I don't know. There's something about him. I can't pinpoint it. Maybe he just has one of those faces."

Yeah, maybe, Matt thought, but somehow, he didn't think that was the case.

"Why didn't you want me to speak to them, Matthew?"

"Because I don't like them," he stated with a tight smile. "And I don't like their methods. Besides, I think your day has been full enough, don't you?"

She closed her eyes, leaned her head back against the headrest. "Yes," she said softly, and with so much defeat, he wanted to pull her into his arms and hold her. Just hold her.

This was not good. What he'd felt when he'd squared off with those two thugs had bordered on predatory. He was not prone to violence, but nothing would have pleased him more than to have shoved a fist into either or both of their ugly faces. He'd overreacted. He'd known it then. He knew it now.

Just as he was overreacting to the look of her. She was pale. She looked fragile and so very vulnerable. Nothing like the aristocratic diva who had graced his table last night with her wide, winning smiles and sparkling wit. As much as he'd enjoyed that woman, as much as he'd wondered what made her tick, he struggled with the gnawing feeling that this woman was the real Helena Reichard and the other was merely a caricature of her true self. Or perhaps they met somewhere in the middle.

No matter. Neither woman was for him. Not now. Not ever.

So why did he feel like he was lying to himself? And why did he feel that he needed to be the one to help her find the common ground between the two?

Grim-faced, Matt watched Helena do little more than shove her food around on her plate later that evening. He was still upset over Yungst and Johannes turning up at the clinic today. He was more upset about the way Helena was acting. "You're very quiet tonight."

They were alone in the dining room. The wine was chilled. So was the conversation.

She'd chosen a pale blue silk pullover sweater tonight. It matched her long, flowing silk skirt. It matched the lovely eyes that he'd been so carefully watching. Eyes that she worked so hard to keep from connecting with his.

She made an attempt to smile, but he could see that her heart wasn't in it. "I'm sorry. I'm not very good company, am I? I must be more tired than I had thought."

"Tired? Yes. And perhaps disappointed with what your doctors had to say today?"

Her startled gaze flashed to his, then away. She blinked, then went back to nudging her food around with her fork, responding to his question with a silence that did very little to guard her uncertainty.

He wasn't sure why he'd knocked on that door. Or maybe he was. He'd gone out on the Web today while she'd rested and searched for information about her. He shouldn't have done it, but he had, and now he knew more about her than he'd wanted to know—and still he didn't know enough.

Dammit, he hadn't wanted to get more deeply involved with her. It wasn't smart. It sure as hell hadn't been on his agenda. And yet, now that the question was out there, he knew he wasn't going to back away. She was suffering, and the pain from her injuries was merely the starting point.

"Do you want to talk about it?" he prodded gently.

She set down the fork, leaned back in her chair and looked at her hands. When she looked up again, her Lady Invincible face was back in place. "Do you think I could learn to drive Lois's golf cart?" she asked in a bright-eyed attempt to evade his questions. "I would so love to browse around the horse barns, but I don't want to bother you. Even though the doctor removed my cast for good today, I'm not sure I could walk that far yet.

"That little chestnut filly," she went on, the animation in her voice not reaching her eyes as she carefully avoided meeting his, "how I'd love to get a better look at her."

Matt listened to her perfect imitation of a carefree prima donna and knew he couldn't let her get by with it any longer. He still wasn't sure when he'd let it get to him, but it was damn near killing him to witness her denial-by-silence that her injuries hadn't affected her life; he couldn't imagine what that denial was doing to her. The thought of the emotional damage she might be doing by refusing to acknowledge or deal with her pain and her new limitations pushed him the final leg home.

"Sure," he said, his voice flat, his expression hard. And right or wrong, wise or foolish, he took the leap and charged into the game like a quarterback calling audibles at the line of scrimmage. "I can teach you to drive the cart. For a price."

She blinked at him. The surprise in her eyes was real, but the playful smile she quickly glued in place was clearly a fabrication. "A price now, is it?"

He nodded. "A big one. Very high ticket."

She studied his face then grew silent, as if she suddenly understood what he was about to ask of her and didn't want to play anymore.

"Perhaps we will talk about this tomorrow," she suggested, her expression carefully guarded as she touched her napkin to the corner of her mouth then laid it beside her plate. "I find I'm actually quite weary."

"Not tomorrow." Ignoring the slight trembling of her hand, he made himself press her. "Now."

After she got past the astonishment at his response, a practiced moue and a little shake of her head relayed what she wanted him to see. Tolerant distaste and one-hundred-fifty-percent avoidance. "Really, Matthew. It does not become you—this sudden lack of gallantry."

"Like your scars don't become you?"

The silence of her shock fell like an anvil.

Long, stunned moments passed before her gaze searched his, dazed and hurt. And then, the panic set in. He watched it spread across her face like a bad dream.

Looking cornered and ready to run, she somehow managed to maintain control as she shoved back from the table.

"No." He gripped the arms of her chair and stopped her when she would have stood and left the room. "You need to talk about this."

Incensed and pale, she met his eyes. "I will not talk about it."

She was trembling with the effort to hide the fear.

"Helena," he said softly.

Wild eyes met his and whatever she saw there made her go utterly still. All the fight seemed to drain out of her. Only her breathing, shallow and rapid, taxed the edgy silence as she stared at a point past his shoulder. And still she held her silence.

"Talk to me, Helena. Tell me. Tell me what happened today that upset you."

She closed her eyes, but not before a tear welled up, spilled over and trickled slowly down her cheek.

Oh, man. He felt like a hand had punched through his ribs and fisted around his heart. But he wasn't backing off. She needed to vent. She needed to let it out. No matter how much of a bully he felt like at the moment, he wasn't going to let her run away from her feelings.

He swallowed hard. "Tell me."

"You don't want to hear." Her voice was barely a whisper, carefully modulated to appear void of emotion. "You don't want to know."

"What don't I want to hear?" he asked softly. "*Why* don't I want to know?"

Her gaze darted to his then away, as if she was ashamed. "Because you will hate me."

Her words were filled with such utter despair that he physically ached for her. "I will hate you?"

"Because I am weak." She looked at her hands, blinking hard to combat the moisture brimming in her eyes, thickening her lashes.

He thought of the times in the hospital when he'd seen her struggle in silence during painful physical therapy, of the smiling face she'd shown the world, her solitary tears when she'd thought no one was watching. He thought of all the things that he'd learned about her this afternoon while she'd slept. The Web had proven to be a fount of information about Lady Helena Reichard that he never would have suspected.

She may have only been in his home for two days, but he'd been learning to know her for two months. "Of one thing, I can assure you," he said gently, "I will never think of you as weak."

Twin teardrops spilled, then stained the blue silk of her skirt. "That's because you don't know me."

"And what would you have me know about you?" he asked gently.

When she didn't answer, he tried a little baiting to see if he could elicit with ruthlessness what he hadn't been able to accomplish with understanding.

"That you are the quintessential blue-blooded do-gooder? That in every aspect of your life, you appear to be a noble earl's daughter who happily lives in a world of events and society functions I will never understand?"

When her gaze shot to his, defensive and angry, he pressed for more. "The paparazzi have proclaimed you the Beautiful Lady of Lost Causes. It seems a fitting title," he said thoughtfully, still hoping to provoke a stronger response. When none came, he responded for her.

"If there's a cause, it appears you champion it. If there's a need, you organize a drive and raise the money for it. Is it a role you enjoy—or do you do it because you were born to it?"

Emotion flared in her eyes and she bristled with an anger he much preferred to her silence. "It would appear that the cynic in you has already decided," she said coldly.

"Ah, yes. The cynic. How does this conclusion fit then? You do all of this because it's the cool, 'in thing' for titled Europeans to attach themselves to one worthy cause or another, correct?"

Her blue eyes frosted over. "Well, there, you see? You have me all figured out." She squared her shoulders, lifted her chin. "Now please excuse me."

"I *thought* I had you figured out," he continued, ignoring her pointed desire to leave. "I had you pegged as the garden-club, museum-renovation, art-restoration type—

and I'd been right. To a point. It seems you also specialize in raising money for homelessness and world hunger.''

She looked down her patrician little nose at him, then nailed him with point-blank sarcasm. ''How horrible of me.''

He smiled sadly. ''How horrible that you choose to keep that part of yourself in such low profile.''

''Is there a point to all of this?'' she asked, seeming to draw on all of her resources to appear bored—when, in fact, he could see that she was anything but bored. She was frightened. Scared right down to her little ballerina slippers of being found out.

''A point? Yes, Helena, I've got a point. The point is, I want you to admit how much your injuries are going to affect your life so you can start to deal with them. I want you to admit that it's hard to find justice in your suffering when you have done so much to alleviate the suffering of others.''

Nothing. Not so much as a flicker of the eyelashes that were still spiked with tears she refused to shed.

''Dammit, Helena, it makes me mad as hell to see you this way—you should be mad as hell, too. And you shouldn't feel diminished to admit it.''

She sat as silent as a stone.

He drew a deep breath, let it out, thought of the numerous articles and photos featuring both her philanthropic works and her playtime—and of the surprises that kept turning up. He'd expected that a woman who looked like her would have a very active love life. Unless she'd managed to be very discreet—a tough trick the way the press hounded her—there didn't seem to be many men in her life, at least not for any long stretch at a time. That information, too, had been interesting—and a little too satisfying. Just as intriguing was his impression that while she'd smiled openly and readily for the cameras, her eyes had always seemed very private and very proud.

Like now.

"You were an athlete and a risk taker," he continued. "You'd skied the Alps' most treacherous slopes, snorkeled uncharted reefs, climbed obscure mountain peaks. You love dressage and steeplechase."

The online photos had clearly shown that the equestrian events were her passion. She'd competed with a great love of the sport if the brilliant smile she wore in all of her photographs was any indication.

"You may never do those things again, and yet you sit there, silent to the pain."

He looked from her hand to her face. Her eyes were blank, all the emotion she refused to let break through banked up behind them again.

"So the point," he restated carefully, "is that I want to know how you can do that."

"It seems that you already know more than enough about me."

"About what you do? Yes. About who you are? No. Does anyone know, Helena? Do you even know who you are?" he asked as that unexpected, but crystal-clear insight into the root of her dilemma swept over him.

The abrupt difference in her demeanor was remarkable. In the space of a shallow breath, he watched her shaky fabrication of a brave front crumble like a sand castle. He could see in her eyes that she wanted to hate him in that moment. She wanted to hate him for forcing her to confront things no one had yet forced her to face.

She drew a deep breath, looked at the ceiling. "Why are you being so cruel? You and Justin. You think I need to talk about my—my injuries as if that will make everything go away."

"And you think ignoring them will?"

"Yes. Yes!" she shouted and shot wildly out of the chair.

He rose, too, reaching out to steady her when she lost her balance. She fought against his hold. In her eyes shone the fact that she was mortified by her outburst even as she was ruled by it. The tears that welled up finally spilled over, breaking her pride, crumbling her defenses.

"Leave me alone. Please, just let…me…go," she cried, not realizing that she was sobbing uncontrollably now.

And then she just gave it up. She gave in. She no longer seemed to care that she was beating futilely against his broad shoulders, that she was crying without shame.

He took each blow without flinching, then, afraid she would hurt herself, pinned her hard against him. He cradled her to his chest, wanting to shelter her from the pain, to hold her together so she wouldn't shatter into a million splintering pieces.

"Shh," he murmured against her hair. "Shush now. You're okay. I've got you."

He'd expected tears. He'd thought he'd been prepared for them. Jena had used tears as weapons against him. She'd turned them on and off like a light switch. He'd soon become immune to her tantrums. But this…this he wasn't equipped to handle.

These tears poured from Helena's soul. They bled from a heart that was slowly breaking.

And it tore him apart as she finally let go, helpless to stop the emotions that poured out and spilled in salty tears to dampen his shirt.

His hands moved to her hair, to gentle and soothe, to caress and care. He whispered her name, tipped her face to his, pressed his lips to her tear-streaked cheeks, a tender intimacy, a healing balm. Her breath fanned his face, warm and wine-scented, and when she pressed her sweet body against his as if she wanted to crawl inside him, something in him shifted. Something profound, something soul-deep and totally encompassing.

He was able to catch the breath that had stalled and filled his chest to bursting—but his mind—his mind, he lost completely.

With a whispered apology and a groan of utter defeat, he sought her mouth with his, covered it. And then he was as lost as she was to anything but the moment and the wonder of her lips opening beneath his.

Seven

Helena caught her breath on a sob and melted into him. Into his touch that was healing, into his heat that was inflaming. She clung to him, opened for him when his tongue coaxed her lips apart.

A groan rumbled from low in his throat. She shivered as he deepened the kiss, opening his mouth wider as if he would devour her, as if he fed on her as a starving man would draw sustenance from sun-ripened fruit. But she knew that she was feeding from him and the comfort he offered. She let herself drown in him and the dark, demanding need his kisses fostered. And what they fostered was complete and healing oblivion.

She'd known his kisses would be like this. She'd dreamed they would be like this. And yet her dreams could not compare to the reality that was Matthew Walker's mouth.

Consuming, commanding, demanding yet giving, he

took her under. She sank willingly with him into the depths.

She'd known his body would be heat and energy and his muscled back hard and lean beneath her hands. She'd known she wanted him. She hadn't known, hadn't dared to dream that he wanted her. But from the moment he'd pulled her into his arms and his big body had shuddered with desire, she'd known that no man had ever made her feel so needed or so alive.

Too few sensual moments had passed when he ended the kiss. He pressed his forehead to hers, closed his eyes, and dragged in a labored breath. "I'm sorry," he murmured even as he wrapped her tighter in his arms. Then he laughed and swore under his breath. "The hell I am. I'm sorry if I hurt you, but I'm not sorry that I kissed you. I don't know what that makes me. I only know that I've wanted to do that since the moment I saw you."

She pulled back, blinked up at him.

He groaned again, lowered his head to press his cheek against the crown of her head. "Please don't look at me like that—not unless you want to finish what we just started."

Her heart slammed hard against her breast. This was too much to believe. Too much to hope for.

She pressed her nose against the hollow at his throat, steeped her confidence in the intimate scent of him, the heat of him. "What were we starting, Matthew?" she whispered into a silence charged with a desperate anticipation that begged him to make her believe.

The sound he made was part laugh, part groan. "My dear lady, if you don't know, then I've got to do some serious reevaluation of my technique."

"Do not joke with me, Matthew," she demanded, pulling back to look into his eyes as hers stung with the insistent, niggling fear that it was compassion, not passion that had prompted his kiss.

He tipped back his head, drew a bracing breath. When he met her eyes again, his were slumberous and dark. "Does this feel like a joke?" He lowered his hands to her hips and pulled her hard against him. His erection pressed full and heavy against the hollow of her hip.

"Matthew," she murmured as he swept her off her feet and into his arms.

"Don't think for a minute that you're off the hook," he warned her gruffly. "You will talk to me. Later," he assured her, just before he lowered his mouth for a kiss that would have buckled her knees had he not been holding her.

She couldn't think for the sweet reassuring certainty that he wanted her. Couldn't breathe for her need of him as he carried her up the broad, sweeping stairway then strode straight past her room.

"Tell me now, Helena," he demanded with an urgency that hurried her heart when he stopped outside the door to his bedroom. "Tell me now if you don't want this."

The intensity of his desire chased away the last of her fears, banished into nonexistence her doubt.

"Talk to me, Helena. Tell me now, Helena." The teasing huskiness in her voice translated to her newfound confidence as she cupped the back of his head in her right hand and pulled his mouth down to hers. "Is that all you Texans know how to do? Talk?"

His wonderful mouth curved into a slow, utterly male smile against hers. "Oh, we talk all right. But we also deliver. The question is—does that titled little mouth of yours know anything about begging? No?" He kicked open the door and strode toward the bed. "Then it's past time you learned."

Her senses were completely immersed in him, in this man whose heart beat like thunder against the curve of her left breast. This man whose strong arms held her against his chest, whose belt buckle bit into her hip like a brand of possession.

Despite her dazed and shimmering excitement, she registered vague impressions of a spacious, masculine room. A towering pine armoire stood against a far wall. The same gleaming floors as in her bedroom were scattered with boldly patterned rugs. Tall, arching windows captured the moon and summoned the night.

His bed stood in a pool of moonlight like an invitation that filled her with an edgy thrill and an aching expectancy.

The intimacy was astounding, as was the sudden realization that what no one but her doctors and her therapists had seen, this man would soon see—this magnificent, perfectly formed man who even now, seemed to read her mind and recognize the reticence she did not want to succumb to.

He set her carefully on the floor, kissed her long and deep with a devastating assault of lips and tongue and teeth. Dizzy with desire, she held on to him for balance as, with a flick of his hand, he tossed back the coverlet then reached for the bedside light.

Instantly tense, she touched her right hand to his, wrapped her fingers around his wrist. "Please. Leave it off."

He studied her face with hooded eyes. "This is where the trust between us ends then?"

She looked away as want and apprehension filled her chest, brought another damnable threat of tears to her eyes.

"I want you, Helena." He lifted her left hand, cloaked in the protective mesh glove, to his lips. "It's that simple."

A single, hot tear spilled down her cheek. "I don't want to be like this. I don't want to be a coward."

He molded her open palm to his cheek, covered it with his hand then turned his face and pressed the most tender of kisses there. "You are the furthest from a coward of anyone I know. You're just a little afraid. A million miles of difference lies between the two."

The look in his eyes touched her deeply. He believed in her. He believed when she could not, and that knowledge both shamed and empowered her.

She drew in a breath. Let it out. She could be brave. For him. She could be strong. For him.

She reached down and with a trembling hand, turned on the light.

"So," she said, with barely a tremor in her voice, "let's get down to the begging part, shall we?"

He smiled then. One of those slow, unfurling smiles that did incredible, wonderful things to her tummy and helped her forget what she no longer was.

When he reached for the hem of her sweater and lifted it over her head, she shivered, as much in anticipation as with apprehension. And when she stood before him in the soft, watery blue silk of her camisole and French-cut panties, she blocked the scars and imperfections from her mind and became what he wanted her to be. A woman who desperately wanted this man.

A sigh slipped through her parted lips as he covered her breasts with his hands and lifted.

"I should have known." He bent to her and caressed her with the heat of his breath, the brush of his lips, the stroking wetness of his tongue. "More silk beneath all that silk."

He slowly slid the straps of her camisole down her arms.

Blue lace caught on the fullness of her breasts, just above her nipples. Beneath the translucent silk, they pearled in wanton invitation as the night air and his warm breath stroked her skin. She caught her breath on a jerky little sigh when he went down on one knee before her.

Sweet, sharp sensations tangled inside her chest as she watched him bury his face between her breasts and gently nuzzle then nudge the lace lower, until he'd bared her to the night and to his mouth.

"Oh." She clutched at his shoulders as he nipped with his lips, rimmed the areola with a circular sweep of his tongue, then caught hold with his teeth and gently tugged. Delicious, curling heat pooled low in her belly. "Oh...my."

She felt his smile against her skin, then the heat of his hands as he tunneled under the camisole to caress her naked flesh.

"Oh," his murmuring echo stroked her skin as he squeezed gently, thumbed her erect nipples still wet from his mouth until she arched into his hands. "Oh...my."

Despite the intense sensuality of the moment, a throaty laugh bubbled out. She smiled down into devil-green eyes. "How do you know how to make me laugh?"

"The same way I know how to make you moan." It was a promise cloaked in a husky growl as his work-roughened hands skimmed down the length of her ribs, his fingers tracking as if he were memorizing every inch of her.

His mouth followed their slow descent in an agonizingly wonderful exploration. He pressed his face into the hollow of her navel, breathing warmth, trailing fire. Hooking his thumbs in the lace of her panties, he slid them carefully down her legs.

She did moan then and unaware, tangled a hand in his dark curls when his mouth moved lower still, licking and nipping a sizzling path to that part of her that pulsed with need, ached with want.

She sucked in a sharp breath when he touched her there. With his lips, with his tongue he made love to her, as his hands palmed her cheeks and drew her against his mouth.

"Matthew." She cried his name on a whimper, the hand in his hair curling into a fist.

He drew back reluctantly. Pressing his cheek against her curls, he kneaded her hips with magic hands. "Too much?" His voice was dark and low, his breath hot and intimate.

She couldn't respond. Her breath slipped out on a thready rasp.

"Or maybe too soon," he concluded, kissing her hip point before slowly rising to his feet.

She didn't know if she felt relieved or bereft, wasn't altogether sure how much longer she could stand.

He smiled again, reading her confusion and desire for what it was. "It's all right," he soothed gently. "We're not done with that." His eyes on hers, he cupped her there, where his mouth had been, then slipped a finger slowly inside. "We're not nearly done with that."

His promise was a ragged whisper as he caught her against him then laid her back on his bed.

"If you knew how often I've fantasized about seeing you like this…." He swallowed hard, shook his head as if coming to his senses. "You're sure?" he demanded, his expression suddenly serious.

If she hadn't already been falling in love with him, that question, in that moment, would have turned the tide. He wasn't merely the most fascinating, attractive man she'd ever met, he was also the kindest, the most considerate. And the most heroic.

"I'm sure," she whispered, knowing that's all he needed to hear, accepting that if he couldn't return her love, he did at least care about her. And he did, absolutely, lust for her. For that alone, she would offer him anything. Anything.

Bending over her, one knee digging into the mattress at her hip, he leaned down and kissed her. It went on forever, that kiss. Soft lips, sleek tongue, gentle suction. And still, it wasn't nearly long enough when, with a gentle nip at the corner of her mouth, he pushed up and away, lifting her camisole over her head and tossing it to the floor. "I'll be right back."

Deliciously aroused and surprisingly unselfconscious sprawled naked in his bed, she watched him cross to the bathroom, stunned anew by his beauty—from the expanse of his broad shoulders, to his long powerful legs, the narrow cut of his hips.

When he returned and tossed a handful of foil packets on the bedside table, a jolt of dizzying heat—part thrill, part shock—raced through her body. She looked from the condoms to him, lifted an inquisitive brow.

His smile was slow and utterly male as he undid the top button on his shirt. "So sue me. I'm a Texan. I think big."

"Well," a flush of heat crept to her breasts where his glittering green eyes had settled, "who am I to question that kind of optimism?"

With a grin that was much more wicked than it was nice, he stripped for her. Nothing blatant. Nothing even remotely suggestive—not by design, at any rate. At least, she didn't think it was. Just a slow shrug of his shirt from his broad shoulders, the flip of a snap, the silent glide of a zipper going down—and all the while his eyes burned into hers, promising passion, demanding desire, emptying her mind of everything but him.

The look of him. The heat of him. The taste of him and of herself on his tongue when he lay down beside her and meshed his mouth to hers.

His body was long and hard, wonderfully hot against the length of hers. His hands were gentle, inventive plunderers, his mouth an instrument of sensation that slowly and skillfully destroyed her with pleasure. Pleasure she'd never dreamed existed. Pleasure so consuming, she forgot she was not what she wanted to be and became what he made her. Wanton. Craving. Carnal.

"Here?" he murmured as his big hand and nimble fingers finessed her nipple to aching sensitivity.

She shivered and arched into his palm.

"I'll take that as a yes."

The smile in his voice was as seductive as the fire in his eyes. She sighed his name when his lips replaced his hand and he drew her deep into his mouth.

"Come inside me. Please," she murmured, near desperation as he braced the heel of his hand over her mound and caressed her boldly. "Matthew, please."

He moved over her then, parted her knees with a slow stroke of his hand and settled between her thighs. He was heavy and strong braced above her. He was steel and velvet and huge as he entered her in a long, steady glide.

Her breath eddied out on a low moan. She rose to meet him as her body stretched, surrendered, surrounded.

"Too much?" he murmured through gritted teeth and lay very still, buried deep. A sheen of perspiration had misted across his back where her hand reveled in the strength of steely muscles and satin-smooth skin.

She hooked an ankle over his hips, clenched her inner muscles, and made a soft, desperate little gasping sound.

His response was more growl than groan. "I'll take that as a no."

She smiled. And then because he was so wonderful, she laughed and he was the one gasping.

On a pained breath, he braced up on his elbows, cupped her face in his hands. "Don't do that. Don't laugh or it'll be all over."

She met green eyes that glistened with a hunger so fierce and so true, it brought tears to her eyes. Oh, this man, this beautiful, incredible man. She'd never felt so desired or so devastatingly sexual.

She touched a hand to his face. He turned his mouth to her palm, bit lightly. Eyes locked with his, she threaded her fingers through his hair and brought his head down to hers. With the tip of her tongue, she skimmed the seam of his lips, slipped her tongue inside the wet heat of his mouth and slowly moved her hips. Her breath caught as he withdrew then plunged deep.

"You're so tight."

"It feels good?"

He muttered something unintelligible against her throat. It was her turn to smile. "I'll take that as a yes."

"Just so you take me," he groaned and started moving inside her. "All of me."

She stopped smiling then. She may have even stopped breathing. All of her focus, all of her awareness was centered on the penetrating stroke of his body into hers. He filled her so wholly, moved her so deeply, she lost track of time, lost track of space, and simply indulged in the sharp, searing pleasure that drove her to the edge of oblivion.

She inhaled on a choked sob as his big hands worked beneath her hips and he tilted her higher, increasing the contact, intensifying the sensation until it built to a pressure that screamed for release.

The orgasm ripped through her, as explosive as a lightning strike. Sharp, brilliant, brutally fierce. She cried his name as the force of it coiled, unwound, then slashed again like the velvet bite of a wildly curling whip.

His breath was harsh and labored as he swore her name and thrust deeply one final time. Tensed above her, he groaned from deep in his chest and followed her with a hoarse exhalation to his own turbulent release.

For several long, stunned moments, they lay still, his face buried in the hollow of her throat, her left hand flung above her head, her right clutched loosely in his hair.

"You okay?" he finally managed, the rush of his breath at her throat cooling her heated skin.

She tried for a deep breath, gave it up. "Umm."

His mouth curved into a smile against her neck. "I'll take that as a definite maybe."

When an exhausted laugh escaped her, he hugged her hard, as if he couldn't get enough of her, as if he'd never get enough of her. The warmth his spontaneous display of affection fostered filled her chest like a burst of summer sun.

He started to roll away.

"No." She clung and told herself it wasn't out of desperation. "Don't go."

"I'm not going anywhere," he promised. "But I'm dead weight for you. There," he said after flicking off the light and settling against her right side, one arm hugging her waist, the other pillowing her head. "Better?"

It didn't get any better, she thought, as he nudged his

thigh between her legs and nuzzled his face in the hair at her temple. Blissfully sated, she twined her leg over his and covered his arm with her hand. And there, bound in the loose knot of each other's limbs, she tried to remember when she'd felt this cherished and safe.

Overhead, a ceiling fan spun in slow, lazy circles. The moon washed in through the tall, shutterless windows, bathing the bed and the man in a misty glow.

She took it all in then, each singular detail, every time-suspended element that had cruised by unnoticed in their desperate rush to ease the ache, quench the fire. The luxurious sheets beneath her, now damp from their perspiration. The musky scent of wonderful sex and sated man. The pale line of his hip, the deep tan of his chest where the sun had bronzed his skin. The hair-roughened length of his muscled thigh.

The heat of the hand that had slowly stolen to her breast to cup and caress.

"I thought you were sleeping," she murmured, loving the lazy way he stroked her, pleasantly surprised by the thickening length of his erection growing long and hard again against her hip.

"I should be. *You* should be," he whispered, both apology and arousal thick in his voice.

She turned her face to his, searched his ocean-dark eyes in the moonlit room. "What I should be, what I am, is so very fortunate to have a lover as generous and…oh…" her breath caught on a moan as his hand forayed lower and caressed her still-swollen flesh.

"Optimistic?" he suggested, just before his mouth descended.

His kiss was deep and hungry. His tongue matched the rhythm of his fingers.

"Helena," he uttered her name with a sudden reverence that stalled her heart. "I'm going to try my damnedest to get enough of you."

She didn't know if he'd just made a pledge to her or to himself and when his mouth trailed a path of liquid fire to her breast, she didn't care. She only hoped that she survived long enough to experience all the promises his mouth was making.

She was a beautiful little mess, Matt decided, as he returned to his bedroom with a tray of food and a bottle of wine. Then he tried not to feel so damn smug about the fact that he was the one who had messed her up.

It was a little after 2:00 a.m. He'd awakened hungry and decided he'd better raid the kitchen instead of taking another bite out of her. So he'd shrugged into a navy blue robe, made his way downstairs and rounded up anything and everything he'd thought she might like.

What he liked was the look of her sprawled naked across his bed. The dwindling stack of condoms said less about his self-control than about his optimism and he couldn't stop another smile.

He set the tray filled with an assortment of cheese and crackers, grapes and melon slices on a table by the window, then settled onto one of the two chairs flanking it to simply watch her sleep. She looked so peaceful and so sensual he felt his sex stir again.

Damn. He'd meant what he'd said. He intended to do his damnedest to get enough of her. He hadn't planned on accomplishing that in one night, though he'd certainly given it his all.

So had she, he thought with another little grin. He plucked a grape from the plate and popped it into his mouth. It was sweet and tart and juicy—just like she was—and so far, his bright idea of sating himself on something other than her wasn't working out quite the way he'd planned it.

But then, what had? He hadn't planned on taking her to bed. He hadn't planned on the tumult of feelings she'd elicited with both her tears and her responses to his touch. And he hadn't planned on such an uninhibited, responsive lover.

For all of her worldly sophistication, his fair lady had reacted to his lovemaking with an arresting innocence that had both excited and humbled him. Each time he'd touched her, she'd made him feel like it had been the first time for her. Each tremulous sigh, each gasping moan had sent him to a flash point, driven him to extremes, compelled him to take her higher, love her longer, fill her deeper.

He was more fascinated with her now that he'd finally tasted her essence and felt the warm silk of her body beneath him than he'd been when he'd been able to do little more than fantasize about her. And instead of feeling sated, he felt as if he'd just taken a small nibble out of the exquisite feast that was Helena Reichard.

The soft rustle of sheets told him she was stirring. The sudden rumble of his heart told him he didn't want her waking up alone.

Rising, he crossed to the bed and sat down beside her. She was on her tummy, her blond hair tumbling across her cheek like a tangled silk curtain. He brushed it away from her face. Slowly, she twisted at her waist and rolled to her back, a soft smile tilting lips swollen from his kisses, a pale hip still planted deep in the covers. Moonlight played across her naked breasts, and without thinking about it, his hand moved to play there, too.

"Mmm," she murmured and arched into his touch, raising her arms above her head in pure, primitive abandon.

"Hello," he said softly, loving the way her lips curved up in a slow, sleepy awakening.

"Hi," she whispered back and covered his hand with hers.

"Are you always like this?" Unable to stop himself, he gathered her into his arms and tugged her onto his lap. She curled into him like a kitten, all warm, giving curves and purring contentment.

"Like what?"

"I don't know." He pressed his mouth to her hair, let out a deep breath. "Trusting," he finally settled on and refused to wonder at the sense of contentment the thought of her trusting him so completely promoted.

When she just sighed and yawned and snuggled closer, he closed his eyes against feelings he didn't want to acknowledge, let alone deal with. It was just the sex, he told himself. It was just great, mind-altering sex.

When her stomach made a hungry, growling sound, it gave him an excuse to table that line of thought that could lead him nowhere but into trouble. It also reminded him of his mission and the reason he'd left her in his bed. He set her carefully off his lap, then shrugged out of his robe and draped it over her shoulders.

"I thought you might be hungry." After returning from his closet, wearing a robe that was a twin to the other one, he urged her to her feet. "Come on. I brought food."

With a delicate little yawn, she stood at his urging, then watched like a sleepwalker as he maneuvered her arms into the sleeves of the robe and belted it at her waist. She should have looked ridiculous, lost in the folds of heavy blue velour. Instead, she looked like what she was—thoroughly loved and as sexy as French silk. The thought of those pale plump breasts and all that warm, naked flesh beneath his robe gave him second thoughts about taking her anywhere but back to bed.

Knowing she needed nourishment, he half led, half coaxed her over to the table, sat her down and rolled up her sleeves for her. With the soft light of a bedside lamp lighting the room, he sat down across from her.

"Do I need to force-feed you?" he asked to the head she'd lowered to the table.

When she didn't respond, he poured them each a glass of wine. "I'm starting to feel guilty here, Helena. Maybe I was a little too hard on you?"

She raised her head then, a self-satisfied and endearingly shy little grin lifting one corner of her mouth. She dragged her hair out of her eyes and away from her face. "Darling," her blue eyes, hazy with sleep, still shimmered with latent arousal, "you will never hear me complain about that."

He laughed, shook his head. "Eat," he commanded, "before that smart mouth of yours gets you into trouble. Again."

"Well, we wouldn't want that, now would we?" she returned with another one of those sultry looks, and nibbled on a piece of melon.

No, he told himself, watching her. We wouldn't want that. He met her eyes, knowing his desire for her was obvious. But even more than the desire, more even than the trust she showed him in bed, he wanted her to trust him enough to talk to him. To open up to him the way she might have opened up if her tears hadn't done him in and he'd felt the need to kiss them away.

Evidently, she could read his face better than he could read hers.

"Thank you," she said softly.

He tilted his head, tested the water. "Oh, no. Thank *you*."

She actually blushed. He thought it was adorable.

"I didn't mean that. Although…that—" she added with a wave in the general direction of the bed, "—was definitely wonderful."

She looked at her wine, then at him. "I meant, thank you for what you tried to do."

"I don't want your thanks," he said, suddenly sober. "I want you to open up to me."

She toyed with the stem of her wineglass. "I know. It's…it's just a little frightening to say some things out loud. It…it seems to give them more import, somehow."

"And that's bad?"

She shook her head. "I don't know. Maybe. All right, yes. I think maybe it is."

"Why don't you try it out—let me help you decide."

She tugged her lower lip between her teeth, an oddly endearing and openly telling indication of how vulnerable she felt.

He watched her nibble delicately on a slice of cheese. This had to be her choice. This had to be her decision to extend the next overture of trust.

He drew in a deep breath. Let it out. He was a fine one to talk about trust. He didn't trust anything he was feeling. Not now. Now as he watched her. Now that he'd made love to her. Now that he'd gotten himself wrapped a little tighter, in a little deeper than he had ever intended—with Helena or any other woman.

It was time to get himself grounded back into some absolutes. He could be her lover and not be in love with her. He could be what she needed tonight and let her go when the time came. And it would come. She had her life to get back to. He had his to maintain. Distance and circumstance and about a thousand years of aristocracy dictated that there would be no middle ground for the two of them. Except perhaps in his bed.

Like most great passions, he knew this one, too, would burn itself out. When it did, and when it was safe for her to leave, he wanted her leaving as his friend. And as her friend, he waited for her to make the next move.

Eight

Helena watched the face of the man who, other than her parents, had given her more than anyone had ever given her. Could he possibly understand what that meant to her? Could he possibly comprehend that in a few short days, in a few short hours, he'd made a major impact on her life? That in his bed, she'd offered him a trust she'd rarely given another man—had never thought she could give to a man again? And the bigger question, would he want the responsibility of knowing that?

Regardless of the intimacies they had shared, she suspected the answer to those questions was no. He was a kind man. A generous man, an unselfish lover. But he didn't love her. He hardly knew her. Still, she felt she knew him, and she knew that he cared. Caring, however, didn't translate to love. It translated to compassion and, in their case, a glorious and mutual lust.

Yet, as he sat there, waiting for whatever she chose to

tell him, she knew that he would understand. Just as he understood her need to expose not only her feelings, but her fears.

How could he know her so well? How could he know what she didn't? That she needed to talk about this, but that fear had kept her from it. Fear and an anger that she'd never understood until he'd made her acknowledge it.

She looked past him, out the window and into the darkness and decided to take that first step. "I may never regain the use of my hand. I may never walk again without a limp."

There. She'd said it. And it hurt every bit as badly as she'd known it would.

Beside her, she heard his long exhalation of breath. "I'm sorry."

She forced a smile. "Me, too. Sorry for the truth of it. Sorry that it took this long for me to accept it. They'd told me that from the beginning. Today, they made me a believer."

Dr. Chambers and Dr. Harding had been kind but graphic as she'd sat listening to the same words she'd heard over and over since the accident. She'd finally been forced to really hear what they were saying.

"With the exception of the donor site on my thigh, most of the burn scars on my leg and arm will fade, the rest can be repaired with cosmetic surgery," she went on, recalling their words. "The muscle tone will gradually return, but the break, well, there was irreparable damage. My hand— plastic surgery after a year or so can improve, but not replicate, what it had once been. Therapy will help me regain some of the use of my fingers but it will be a long painful process."

"Again, I'm sorry," he said softly. When she said nothing, he filled the silence with affirmation. "None of it changes who you are."

She looked up at him. "Well, then, there's the crux of it all, isn't it?" She fussed with the folds of his robe. "You asked me a very insightful question earlier tonight. You asked me who I was. You asked me if I knew who I was. Well, you know what? I don't know. I really don't know anymore. Sometimes...sometimes I wonder if I ever did."

She was grateful that he didn't try to correct her. She was grateful for his silence that allowed her to formulate the words she'd needed to say for a very long time.

"Up until the plane crash," she began hesitantly, trusting him to understand what was just becoming clear to her, "I had always known my purpose. I'd been born to waltz through a charmed, storybook life like a dancer playing to a series of packed houses and standing ovations. I'd been conditioned to believe that the only thing I'd ever needed to trade on was my looks. In fact," she added, unaware that her voice had turned bitter, "it was all that had ever been asked of me. 'Smile for the camera, Helena. Pose for the world. Show them how beautiful you are.'"

She reached for her wine, sipped, stared into the rich burgundy depths. "And I delivered. I played the role and played it well. The mix worked for me. Not only had I been perfect, I'd been perfectly happy. At least I thought I was."

"And now..?" he prompted, after a silence that rejected everything that she had thought.

She looked past him, into the night. "And now," she said, hearing the defeat in her voice but unable to disguise it, "I will never be perfect again."

She met his searching eyes, then looked away from the compassion there and confessed what she had only recently admitted to herself. ''I find myself wondering if I ever truly was.''

The panic started to build again, but this time she didn't hold it in. ''It scares me to death…this realization that my entire identity had been wrapped up in what I looked like. What image I maintained. How shallow is that? And now, how ironic to find, in that sorry assessment, that I was never really perfect after all.''

She looked at him, at the compassion in his eyes. ''And if I was never really perfect, then it makes my entire life a lie, doesn't it?'' she concluded, more frightened than she'd thought possible by the implications of that statement. ''Not a harmful lie, but an empty one, like an empty promise.''

He was quick to defend her. ''You forget. I know too much about you to accept that your life has been an empty promise, Helena.''

She smiled at the kindness and sincerity of his words. ''But don't you see, it's starting to feel that way. I…thought I knew why I did what I did. I thought I was happy. But then, I'd never really stopped to analyze it. I'm wondering now if the reason I never looked any deeper was because I was frightened of the answer even then.''

She laughed, but with no humor. ''God forbid that I'd actually take time for a moment of self-assessment or to delve into that frightening realm of self-discovery. God forbid that I ever asked myself if there was something more to me than what anyone had ever asked me to be.

''What if you were right?'' she asked abruptly. ''Earlier, when you were baiting me—and I know you were baiting me, Matthew—but what if you were right? What if everything I've done until this point was for reasons that were as shallow and superficial as…as a jet-setting daughter of a titled earl?''

He only sat, silent, supportive, listening. She combed her fingers through her hair, fought for the words. "Was that all I was? Was that all there was to me? Shouldn't there have been more? Shouldn't there *be* more?"

She drew in a deep breath, let it out. "I guess I'll never know now, will I? Isn't it odd? My looks had always defined me, and suddenly I find that quite appalling."

She pushed the sleeve away from her hand, stared at the damage. "And now, now I have something new to define me."

She hated the weakness that had tears welling up in her eyes. "I don't want people to look at me and compare me to what I was, when what I was was no less marred than what I am now."

"You are not marred, Helena. You never were. You could have used your position and your beauty for your own personal gain. Instead, you used it to help others."

She nodded slowly. "Oh yes, there is that, isn't there? But now I'll never know what truly motivated me, will I? After all, what I did was all I was equipped to do.

"What am I equipped to do now, Matthew?" she asked, hating the plaintive note to her voice.

"Give it some time. Give yourself some time and you'll find out a lot about yourself if you look deep enough."

She smiled and couldn't keep the cynicism from her voice. "Ah. So I should look at my scars as an opportunity."

"Better that than as a defeat."

"But it's defeat that I feel." The words were out before she could stop them. "For two months I've fought it. What if I never get past it?"

"Again—you haven't given yourself enough time. You aren't giving yourself enough credit."

She didn't know. She just didn't know anymore.

''In the meantime,'' he took her hand and drew her onto his lap, ''why don't you just let yourself get used to the new you, who happens to be someone that I like very much. No,'' he said, cupping her face in his hands, ''you need to think about what you've just said.''

His gaze dropped to the lapels of her robe where it gaped open. ''And I need to do this.''

His hand slipped inside.

She shivered, then leaned into his touch as he filled his palm with her breast.

''What you do to me,'' she whispered, as he lifted her, then shifted her until she was straddling his lap and her arms were looped loosely over his shoulders.

''What do you want me to do to you?'' Eyes locked with hers, he slowly undid the belt at her waist. Slower still, he peeled the robe from her shoulders. It pooled like a deep blue sea at his feet.

''Touch me,'' she uttered on a sigh while she went to work on his belt.

''Like this?'' He repositioned her again so there was nothing between them but skin. His erection pressed against her, hot and heavy.

''Yes,'' she said on a breathless whisper as he lifted her yet again, then brought her down until the tip of his arousal just penetrated her feminine folds.

''More?''

''Umm. More.''

He gripped her hips, pulled her down until he was buried so deeply inside her that she felt him touch her womb.

His eyes on hers, he covered her abdomen with the flat of his palm, pressed. She moaned and clenched around him, her head thrown back, her back arched as she rocked against him, utterly consumed, totally lost to anything but the moment and the magic that only this man could conjure.

He'd been awake for a while. Watching the morning sunlight play across her face while she slept. Indulging in her fragrant warmth beside him, her silken length tangled in his sheets.

It had been a long time since he'd awakened with a woman in his bed. Longer still since he'd wanted to. And when Lois's voice bleated into the silence like a foghorn, he wasn't sure if he was relieved that the spell Helena had woven was broken, or disappointed he hadn't had time to be drawn in a little deeper.

"Matthew Walker, are you gonna sleep all day?"

A glance at the clock on the bedside table beside the intercom told him it was closing in on 8:00 a.m. A glance at the woman who had bolted to a sitting position beside him told him she was closing in on panic.

Her hair was a wild drift of golden silk, her blue eyes startled and still brimming with sleep. She looked frantically around her as if she expected to see Lois peeking up at them from under the bed.

Grinning, Matt reached behind her to punch a button on the intercom. "Good morning to you too, Lois," he said, leaning back on an elbow and taking his time looking over the bare-breasted vixen who had belatedly clutched the sheets to her chin and was looking for all the world as if she'd been caught stealing the family jewels.

"You sick?" Lois demanded.

"No, ma'am." He tugged Helena back down and bent over her, pressing a kiss to the tip of her nose. "Just feeling a little lazy. As a matter of fact," he said, nipping lightly at her chin, "I was thinking about having breakfast in bed."

Lois made a snorting hurmph. "You want breakfast in bed, you'd better start sleeping in the kitchen."

Helena stifled a laugh against his throat, then grinned up at him. He couldn't help it. He bent his head and kissed her, long and slow and thorough.

"Matthew. What's going on up there is what I'd like to know? The countess hasn't been down for breakfast either."

He brushed his thumb along her jaw. "She had a rough day yesterday," he said, having long ago given up on convincing Lois that Helena was not a countess. "I've been helping her with a little physical therapy."

He smothered Helena's gasping laugh with a pillow then sat up, swinging his legs over the side of the bed. "How about you throw some coffee and muffins on a tray and I'll come down and deliver it to her?"

"How about you do that," Lois returned tartly. "But you mind your manners with that lady. Make sure you got everything buttoned and tucked before you give her the shock of her life. She's delicate, she is, and not used to the—"

"Lois. Trust me, okay? I know how to treat a lady."

Behind his back, the lady in question swung a pillow that hit him in the head.

"I'm going to take a shower now," he interrupted when Lois started into a diatribe about no-account pups who wouldn't know a lady if one took and invited them to tea. "I'll be down in about fifteen or twenty. Good-bye, Lois," he ended pointedly and punched the mute button.

"Therapy, now is it?" Helena asked with a demure smile as she tucked a pillow behind her head.

He stood beside her, unabashedly naked, growing aroused just from the look of her all snug and rosy between his sheets. "Well, I for one, definitely found some therapeutic value in what we did last night."

"And again this morning," she added with a pretty blush.

"And let's not discount the healing powers of a hot shower." He scooped her into his arms and carried her into his marble and mirrored bathroom.

"Oh," she said as he set her on her feet and reached in to turn on the spray in a shower stall that could have easily held four people. "By all means, let's not forget about that."

The smile left his eyes when he pulled her in behind him and shut the glass door. Beneath the pulsating mist of multiple showerheads, he bathed her.

Helena's heart swelled with a love so big it hurt. With tender care, he shampooed her hair, paid special attention to the burns on her arm, carefully soaped every inch of her damaged left hand, bent down on one knee to press his mouth to the donor site on her thigh, to caress the surgical scars on either side of her ankle.

"If I could kiss away your pain, I would do it." He rose to his feet and drew her against him.

"You have," she whispered against his shoulder. "You will never know how much you have."

She took the soap from him then, smoothed the rich lather across the beautiful breadth of his chest, along the rock-hard plains of his abdomen and lower, where she took him in her hand, then knelt and took him in her mouth.

"Helena," he ground out her name between clenched teeth as the warm spray poured over them like rain.

"Let me," she whispered against his tumescent flesh as he knotted a hand in her wet hair. "Just let me."

She took the power then, she took control, and she

showed him with her touch the love she couldn't risk putting into words.

Matt stood in the library, watching Helena through the window. She sat on the terrace in the sun, a book lying open on her lap, a glass of Lois's iced chamomile tea, untouched, on the table beside her.

A warm midday breeze caught her hair, lifted it away from her face. The Texas sun had painted her cheeks a becoming pink. And a pain that he felt as if it were his own had tightened her lips, traced fine lines around her eyes.

She wasn't aware that he watched her. In fact, she would be appalled that he'd caught her in this unguarded moment when she was so vulnerable and so open to discovery.

Something in his chest tightened, built to a dull ache as she stared hard at her left hand as if willing the fingers to move into something more than a loose, unnatural fist.

They'd only been lovers for two nights and yet he could read her thoughts, feel her disappointment. She was a wild and generous lover. At night, in his bed, she would shed her inhibitions and become everything she wanted to be. Everything a man could ask for.

But during the day, no matter how hard she tried to hide it, her injuries ruled who she was. It was as she'd confessed to him that first night they'd made love. She didn't want to, but she was letting them define her. She struggled to overcome it daily. In silence. In solitude. She hadn't opened up to him since that night. He hadn't pressed. As he wanted to now.

Instead, he fought the urge to go to her as her shoulders sagged in defeat. Even at this distance he could see that she had closed her eyes against the tears she refused to shed.

He turned away, feeling like an intruder to a very private and very personal struggle. She could only do this on her own. She could only be what she gave herself permission to be. He couldn't fight that battle for her. He didn't have that right.

He eased a hip onto the corner of a desk, cupped his jaw in his palm and reminded himself of a few cold, hard facts. He was her lover, but he wasn't in love with her. Oh, he could easily fall over that edge. He could willingly step over the cliff and take the headlong tumble. But he wouldn't. For her sake as well as his, he would keep his heart out of the equation, because, as tempting as it was, he could not let himself love Helena Reichard.

It wouldn't work. She had a life in Europe she would eventually go back to. He had High Stakes—and the memory of a woman he had once loved, but not enough to make her happy. Granted, he'd come to discover that Helena was nothing like Jena, but the dynamics remained the same. She was born to shine in a world of the socially elite and as soon as her confidence returned, she'd settle comfortably back under that spotlight. He was born with an aversion to the limelight and would never be comfortable there. Their lifestyles simply did not mix.

He also wanted her happy—and if he asked her to stay, to make High Stakes her home, eventually she'd grow tired of Texas. And she'd grow tired of him. Then neither of them would be content.

So, he was willing to settle for what they had, while they had it. In the meantime, he wanted her healed. And he didn't know how much longer he could take seeing her like this. It was a start, but it wasn't enough that she'd identified and accepted that she was letting herself be ruled by her injuries. She needed to start making efforts toward dealing with them.

She wouldn't talk to him about the physical therapy that she did by herself behind her closed bedroom door. She wouldn't admit to the pain even though, as now, he could see it in the fine lines of strain around her mouth. Little by little, he could see it taking a firmer hold on her. Little by little, he could see her giving up and giving in to the idea that she was physically limited in what she could do.

Maybe she *was* limited. Then again, maybe she simply needed someone—or something—other than herself to help her set some new limits.

He rose and turned back toward the window. She'd picked up the book, was trying to lose herself in it, but the way she slowly closed it and stared off toward the horse barns told him she hadn't been successful. Just as he hadn't been successful putting the skids on an idea that had hatched last night after she'd fallen asleep.

He pinched his jaw between his thumb and forefinger, let the air out of his lungs. "What the hell," he said under his breath and decided to go for it.

"Enjoying the sunshine?" Matt asked as he walked out onto the terrace.

Helena's face brightened when she saw him. She graced him with a smile that rivaled the warmth of the sun. "It's lovely."

He braced one hand on the arm of her chair, one on the back and leaned down to kiss her softly on the mouth. "Now *that* was lovely," he said, pulling slowly away.

She actually blushed. He thought it was fascinating.

"Matthew. Lois—"

"—is probably watching, I know. You don't honestly think she doesn't know we're lovers?"

"You...you didn't tell her?" There was more hope in the statement than question.

He smiled. "I didn't have to. She doesn't usually give me wake-up calls every morning—and I've no doubt that as soon as she's checked on me, she makes a quick call to your room. I answer. You don't. It doesn't take a nuclear physicist to do the math on that one."

"Oh, Lord," she said with a dawning realization. "What must she think?"

"Well," he eased close again to take another taste of her full, lush mouth, "we had apricot brandy muffins this morning. Lois has to be in a re-e-al good mood to bake her apricot muffins."

She smiled up at him. "And you seem to be in a re-e-al good mood yourself. What are you about today?"

"I'm about this far from putting my life in your hands." He extended one of his.

She took it and rose. "Your life in my hands? Sounds like the makings of a power trip to me. What did you have in mind?"

He tucked her under his shoulder and started walking slowly toward the house. "I want you to drive me down to the barns."

"Ah. So you want to see firsthand if you were a good instructor?"

He'd taught her to drive Lois's golf cart yesterday. Then he'd let her loose to find her comfort level on her own.

"Something like that." He squeezed her shoulder.

"I warn you, Matthew, I will not tolerate any front-seat drivers," she said playfully. "And I like to go fast."

He chuckled. "Maybe I should drive."

She just laughed. And then she drove. Fast.

"Oh, Matthew, what happened to her?" Helena asked, her voice thick with concern as she stood, her arms crossed over the box-stall door, staring at the injured horse.

For the better part of the last hour, Matt had directed Helena to drive him from one barn to the other. They'd checked on the foals and the yearlings. They'd watched Vince and the boys work the two-year-olds in the round pen. Their last stop was at the west barn. He'd decided it was time for Helena to meet Jewell.

Jewell was a rosy-red roan, a three-year-old athlete bred for speed and agility. She'd been on her way to the top of the cutting horse world when she'd suffered a crippling injury.

"Windstorm about three months ago," he said, watching Helena's face. "She'd just had a workout and was cooling down in the south pen. We're not sure what happened exactly, but she spooked and ran through a fence. It cut her up pretty badly."

"Poor pretty girl," Helena crooned as Jewell stood loafing on her left rear leg, her right rear leg cocked and not bearing any weight. Her liquid brown eyes regarded Helena with a calm interest.

"Will she heal?" she asked softly.

Matt propped an elbow on the stall door. "She'll heal. Question is, will she compete again?"

"What does the vet say?"

He shrugged and, without asking if she wanted to go in, flipped the latch on the stall door and slowly swung it open. "He says it's partly up to her."

Without even realizing she'd made a decision, Helena limped slowly into the stall.

"Hello, pretty girl," she crooned, letting Jewell get used to the sound of her voice, the touch of her hand on her withers. "Let's have a look, okay?"

Matt watched quietly as the small woman spoke in soothing whispers to the thousand-pound horse, who regarded her, if not warily, at least as a curiosity.

He'd given it a lot of thought before finally deciding to bring Helena and the injured quarter horse together. He hoped he hadn't made a mistake. The look in Helena's eyes told him that he hadn't. She was positively maternal with the young mare. Cooing softly, crooning gently, she ran her hand across her withers, testing her trust before she finally extended her exploration to the healing scar on her rear hock.

The mare stood statue-still—except for the slight trembling that vibrated through her entire body.

"Oh, sweet girl, it's all right. No one's going to hurt you," Helena murmured softly, her movements slow and calculated so as not to startle the horse. She worked her way back to the mare's head then scratched her ears and whispered sweet nothings.

"She seems scared to death." Her brows furrowed as she lifted questioning eyes to Matt.

"It's the damnedest thing. Doc says she should be past the memory by now, and past the worst of the pain. But she refuses to put any weight on that leg and she tenses up any time anyone tries to work with her."

"She's still frightened," Helena said in the little roan's defense.

"Either that, or the injury broke her spirit."

Helena's gaze met his, her eyes carefully blank. "What will happen to her?"

He shook his head. "I don't know. She loved to compete. And man, was she a natural." He thumbed back his charcoal Stetson. "If she doesn't come out of it, I suppose she'll end up a broodmare."

The furrow between Helena's eyes deepened. "Maybe she just needs a little special attention."

Matt looked away, contained the smile that had been tugging at the corner of his mouth. He cleared his throat, turned back with a sober frown. "Maybe. Trouble is, we're getting ready for a big competition. I can't spare the hands."

She gave the mare one last pat on the withers, her hand gliding down her glistening coat in a way that told him she was reluctant to leave her.

"A shame," she said thoughtfully and walked slowly from the stall.

"Yeah," he said, "it's a damn shame."

She was unusually quiet that evening. And when they made love, it was with a tenderness that left him humbled and in awe of her capacity for giving.

The next morning, he left her sleeping and went directly to the barns. When he came back to the house for lunch, she wasn't there.

"Took the cart," Lois said when he ended up in the kitchen asking if Lois knew where Helena was. "Said she was heading for the barn and she was dressed in a pair of Becca's jeans and some soft boots. She asked me to take and braid her hair," Lois said, beaming. "Imagine. Me, braiding a countess's hair. Like silk, it was," she went on, ignoring, as always, Matt's grinning attempt to correct her concerning Helena's title.

"But then I guess you'd know all about that, wouldn't you?" she added, her old eyes watching him in a way that made him decidedly uncomfortable.

"The barn, huh?" was all he said as he walked to the refrigerator and snagged a can of soda.

"She's not like Jena, Matthew," Lois said softly. "Be a shame if you took and let her get away."

He stiffened, then turned slowly toward her. "She's my guest, Lois. When it's time, she'll leave. She has a life to go back to. And I have one to maintain."

Lois didn't say anything. She didn't even snort. She just

wiped her hands on her apron, gave him a long look and turned back to the stove and the pots simmering on the front burners.

When he reached the barn where Jewell was stalled, he found Lois's cart in the middle of the alley and Helena, her back to him, on the cell phone.

He stood quietly in the shadows, when what he wanted to do was turn her into his arms. He wanted to fill his palms with her beautiful little backside that was packed into those skin-tight Wranglers. Then he wanted to haul her up to the loft and peel her out of both the jeans and the flannel shirt she'd tucked into them. Afterwards, he wanted to lie in the hay and pick twigs of sweet clover out of the braid that he had thoroughly ruined with his hands.

But what he did was back quietly away when he heard her discussing Jewell's injury and possible treatment with his on-call vet. She was resourceful, he thought with a grin and wondered who she'd cornered long enough to get Doc Jones's number.

Was he worried that Helena was biting off a little more than she could chew by getting wrapped up in Jewell's recovery? Hell yes. Was he concerned that if Jewell didn't respond to her attention she would see it as a sign that neither of them were destined to improve? Damn right.

But as the days passed and Helena became more involved with Jewell's rehabilitation, he could see that he'd been right to plant the seed that had brought them together. As he sat across from her at dinner each evening and saw the sparkle return to her eyes, saw an animation in her expression that made her look younger and centered and confident, he decided it was worth the risk. And he didn't feel even a twinge of guilt over manipulating her into that situation.

As he'd hoped, Helena had begun to see something of herself in the injured mare. From all indications, pitting her own limitations against Jewell's had given Helena a purpose and a goal. If Jewell could get past her injuries, then so, perhaps, could she. If Jewell could compete again, so, perhaps, could she.

As the days passed, she completely immersed herself in Jewell's care. She took over the daily task of changing her dressings, massaging her damaged muscles, coaxing her to absorb some of her weight on that leg. Little by little Jewell began to accept Helena's prompting.

When Matt came upon them—and he made it a point to check on them several times a day—it was a sight that never failed to cause a heart-deep ache in his chest. The beautiful, injured woman, the sleek, crippled horse. Both of them dealing with the damage, both in pain, both valiantly trying to work through the exercise-therapy program Matt's vet had prescribed.

"'What wound did ever heal but by degrees?'" he whispered against her hair when he found her late one afternoon, exhausted and frustrated by her own limitations and Jewell's painfully slow progress.

He hadn't meant to make her cry. But there were tears streaming down her cheeks as she snuggled in his arms and smiled up at him. "Not only is he kind and sensitive, but he quotes Shakespeare," she said around a watery laugh. "However is a girl supposed to resist you, Matthew Walker?"

"Many have tried," he teased gently, "but few have succeeded."

"And he's humble, too." With a bracing breath, she pulled slowly out of his arms. "Now that you've shored me up, go away. I've got work to do."

He kept a loose grip on her arms. "Don't push too hard, okay?"

"It's past time I did a little pushing." She touched a hand to his cheek. "Now, go. Don't worry about me."

But he did worry, as well as marvel at her patience and her drive. He didn't know if she was aware of the change, but little by little, he could see improvement in the mobility in both her hand and her ankle. Her limp seemed less pronounced. She used her left hand with less reluctance.

It was an amazing transformation to watch. And it cemented into fact that although she may think she needed him now, she was finding her own strength again. And as she grew stronger, she would soon be ready to move on. He knew she was very fond of him. He suspected she might even be a little in love with him. But he knew it would pass, just as he'd be ready to let her go when she was ready to move back into her world and out of his.

And he *would* be ready, he told himself, ignoring the dull ache the thought never failed to resurrect to sit like lead in his gut.

Nine

It had been a full three weeks since she'd arrived at High Stakes, Helena thought reflectively, as she relaxed, naked, in the huge whirlpool tub sunk in the floor of Matthew's bathroom. She'd been working with Jewell for seventeen days. She'd been back to the doctor two more times and, thanks to Aaron and Pamela's kindness and Matt's determination to keep her trips into Royal low-profile, she'd managed to evade the press each time.

She'd talked with her parents twice, most recently just last night, assuring them that she was fine then making them laugh at her tales of Texas and her experience on a working ranch.

"How wonderfully quaint, dear," her mother had said with a smile in her voice. "And how hospitable of your friend Mr. Walker to give you this dazzling taste of Americana."

She smiled at the memory of the call—and at her hospitable friend, Mr. Walker, who was currently sitting across from her—also naked—in the whirlpool. His eyes were closed, his head lay back, his bronzed arms were stretched out across the rim of the sunken tub. He did not look quaint. He did, however, look dazzling. And positively wicked. And so gorgeous, her heart stalled.

Water beaded like transparent pearls across the sinewy breadth of his shoulders, clung to his dark, wet curls, trickled in a slow, enticing river from his temple to his jaw before disappearing in the hollow of his throat.

"Something on your mind, Lady Helena?"

Her gaze rose to his to find him watching her through heavy-lidded eyes. His tone was deceptively casual, absolutely sexual.

"Why don't you come over here and ask me that question, cowboy?"

His smile started at one corner of his mouth, slow but not at all sweet as he sat forward, raked both hands through his wet hair and shoved away from the wall of the tub. He cut through the water then braced his hands on the lip of the tub on either side of her head. "Something on your mind?" he repeated against her lips.

"Umm, actually," she murmured, pressing soft, eating kisses to his chin, to his jaw, then licking a line from his throat to his mouth, "I was wondering if you tasted as good as you looked."

He moved in closer, brushing his chest against her breasts. "And…?"

She shivered despite the heat of the water. "You most definitely do."

He smiled as his hands moved to cover her breasts. Watching her eyes, he scraped his thumbnails across her nipples. She caught her breath on a shallow little hitch as he lifted her until her breasts cleared the waterline. "I've been wanting a little taste myself."

Warm, churning bubbles lapped at the underside of her breasts as his soft, wet mouth surrounded her, drawing her deep.

"Matthew." She cried his name on a sigh and arched into his mouth.

"Not enough," he murmured, nuzzling her with his nose, nipping her slick flesh lightly.

His eyes were very dark as he lifted her out of the water and set her on the floor surrounding the tub. Dripping wet, he rose in front of her, snagged a stack of towels and spread them out on the floor behind her. Then he laid her down on the bed he'd made of plush terrycloth.

"Not nearly enough," he whispered as he sank back down in the water and moved between her legs. Liquid with anticipation, she raised up on her elbows to watch his beautiful face as he kissed the inside of her right thigh and then her left before he draped her legs over his shoulders.

"Not. Nearly. Enough."

At the first touch of his mouth she whispered his name. At the first stroke of his tongue, she cried out, then surrendered, gave herself over completely to a pleasure so electric it shot lapping flames screaming through her blood. She embraced the shock of it, let it consume her, let him destroy her until she was boneless and whimpering his name, utterly helpless, totally without shame.

She was still coming down when he dragged her back into the water. His mouth sought hers, hard and demanding as he wrapped her in his arms and turned them so his back was against the tub's wall. In one silken stroke, he filled her, making her his with each deep thrust, taking her higher than she'd ever been in a wet, wild rush.

He clenched his jaw, closed his eyes and exploded inside her with a low, guttural groan and shot her over yet another edge of sensation so shattering, she wasn't sure she'd survive it.

"Helena," he groaned her name against her throat as she floated on the edge of consciousness. "Helena." An accolade, a surrender. "What you do to me."

She lay against him, as limp as her wet hair, knowing and not really caring that she would surely drown if he weren't holding her above the water.

Long moments passed as they clung to each other that way. The timer on the jets finally shut off, leaving the room thick with steam and the water still but for their ragged breathing.

"I swear," he ran a hand down the length of her wet hair, "I really, truly had your welfare in mind when I suggested the hot tub."

She smiled lazily against his shoulder. "Darling, you saw to my welfare just fine."

He chuckled. "I meant, I was thinking of the Jacuzzi in terms of honest-to-goodness physical therapy."

With what strength she had left, she pulled away and smiled into his beautiful green eyes, their thick lashes spiked with water. She brushed a wet, unruly curl away from his forehead. "If it will soothe your conscience, I feel very little stiffness in my ankle right about now."

"Oh yeah?" That crooked grin crawled back up one side of his mouth.

"Oh yeah." She collapsed against him again, sleepily murmured, "I don't suppose we could schedule another therapy session for tomorrow? Same time? Same place?"

He hugged her hard. "I guess that depends on whether we drown in here tonight. We need to get out, but I don't know if I can walk."

"Really?"

"You don't have to sound so smug."

"Oh, but smug is exactly how I feel."

And love. Love was exactly what she felt for this giving man who had shown her a side of herself, a sensual side, that she hadn't known existed.

Only later, after they'd managed to stumble to bed and he'd fallen asleep in her arms, did she let herself think about her feelings for him.

It was something she'd purposely never talked about with Matthew. It was, after all, quite gauche of her to have fallen in love with him. Or so her friends would say. They took lovers. They did not fall in love with them. That was not the expectation.

Matthew did not have expectations either. She knew he cared for her. Maybe even more than a little. But not enough to ask her to be a part of his life.

He stirred beside her, drew her tighter against his side in his sleep. She trailed her hand lovingly through his hair, knowing he was so deeply asleep nothing would wake him. Love like this, intimacy like this had eluded her for her entire life. By choice or by design, she wasn't really sure which. It had simply been…easier to maintain distance. To avoid any intense relationships. Or perhaps she had simply never met anyone who had moved her enough to explore the possibilities.

Until now.

She stared into the dark, wishing there could be possibilities for them. Possibilities with this beautiful man, a man she was profoundly attracted to. This man who made her want to look a little deeper, who made her yearn to know if there was more to her, if she had more to give. To a relationship. To one special person, instead of maintaining a careful distance from the world at large.

The world at large. Her hand stilled in his hair. The

world was the bigger picture. She had to keep that in sight. His world and hers did not mix. She thought back to their first dinner together and how he'd rejected her comment that she could grow to love Texas.

...my experience with beautiful women is that they prefer civilization and cities...to solitude and breathtaking sunsets.

She'd wondered then about the women in his life. Wondered if, perhaps, there had been one woman who had disappointed him. But she'd never asked and he'd never offered. He rarely offered anything about himself. It stung. But it effectively drew a line he didn't want to cross.

He had been wrong, though, about what she preferred. Even now, knowing the time would come, she felt too much regret over the thought of leaving High Stakes. It was unsettling this...this almost instant connection she'd felt for his home. It was more than the stark, harsh beauty of the endless desert and the lush opulence of the house and grounds. More than the comfort. Even more than the company. She couldn't suppress the notion that it seemed, somehow, like the perfect hideout. From the press. Perhaps from her own insecurities.

And there, Helena, is the rest of the story. While she knew her feelings for Matthew were strong, she suspected that they were somehow tangled up in her fear of facing the world again. Maybe he suspected it, too. He made it very convenient to settle in here but at the same time was very careful not to attach any expectations.

It would probably be best for all concerned when she finally found her courage and put some distance between herself and this man who, in the span of a few short weeks, had made her think about things she'd never thought about before. Things like belonging...to someone. Needing... someone.

Soon, she promised herself as she indulged in the solid warmth of his body wrapped around her. Soon, she would find that facet of herself that wanted to play for the camera, smile for the world. And when she did, it would be time to leave him.

But not tonight. Tonight, she'd found everything she'd ever wanted in the arms of this beautiful Texan who held her.

"Look, I told you. I'll get in touch when the lady is ready to talk to you. Yeah. I've got your number."

Matt slammed down the receiver. Only after he'd muttered a few choice words beneath his breath, did he realize he had an audience.

"Oh. Hi." He crossed his arms over his chest and leaned a hip against his desk when he turned and found Helena standing hesitantly in the doorway of his office.

She looked from the phone to him. "Who was that on the phone, Matthew?"

He thought about lying to her, but there was really little point; he couldn't protect her from this meeting forever. "Remember those two men who stopped us after your first clinic visit?"

"The investigators from Asterland."

He nodded. "They still want to talk to you."

She leaned a shoulder against the doorframe. "About the crash."

Although her face was blank of emotion, he could tell from the tone of her voice that the idea bothered her. "You don't have to do it, Helena."

She met his eyes. "Maybe it's time that I do."

He looked at the tips of his boots, clenched his jaw but said nothing.

She walked up beside him and picked up the morning

edition of the Royal paper that lay on his desk. While she was no longer the headline material of past editions, there was still an article about her on the front page along with speculations about her whereabouts. "It's time I talk with the press, too," she added and tossed it back down.

Matt looked into the eyes of the woman who had been released from the hospital a little over three weeks ago. That woman, for all of her practiced airs, would never have been strong enough to face the press or Yungst and Johannes. A different woman faced him now. A woman who was rediscovering her own strengths and was ready to test them. He found both relief and regret in that knowledge. He was glad for her. Glad she had rallied to this level of confidence, yet unaccountably upset that it meant the beginning of the end of their time together at High Stakes. The thought tweaked more than it should have, even though he'd known all along that she would eventually leave.

"It's your call," he said carefully. "But if you decide to do it, it'll be by my rules."

She regarded him with questioning eyes.

"I'll call a press conference. We'll hold it here. That way I can control when they come, when they go, and how many. We'll invite Yungst and Johannes and get it over with in one big party."

"I can't allow you to let them invade your home. You have no idea the circus this will turn into."

He smiled ruefully. "I got a pretty good idea the day you were released from the hospital. I won't let them mob you. This will be on my terms, on my turf."

She walked over to him, placed a soft kiss on the firm line of his mouth. "My brave Texas knight. You would hold off a legion of enemies for me, wouldn't you?"

He said nothing, but he realized in that moment that he would do exactly that.

She shook her head. "Matthew, listen to me. Once the press knows where I am, they will camp out on your doorstep like gypsies. Pictures of your ranch will be printed all over the world. They'll fly over in helicopters; they'll perch in your trees. They'll do anything to get to me and, by association, to you. Your life will be forever altered. Your privacy will be destroyed. I don't want that to happen to you."

She was right. He'd known it when he'd made his ultimatum and still he'd been determined to go through with it. More than he was concerned about his privacy, however, he was concerned about her safety. She still didn't know her life might be in jeopardy. And he still wasn't willing to put her at risk. Here, at High Stakes, he could control the elements. He had good men working for him. Loyal men. But, there were only so many of them and he had no idea what kind of odds he was up against.

"Okay," he said, reconsidering. "We won't do it here. Give me a couple of days and I'll get something worked out."

"Why not hold the conference at the hotel?" she suggested. "It's very public, and yet I'm sure the staff would arrange for my privacy."

The hotel *was* very public. Too public. Too many things could go wrong.

"I'll think about it," he said evasively. "Just trust me to handle this for you, okay?"

"I trust you, Matthew," she said and stepped away. "I have always trusted you."

And then she walked out the door.

He didn't know why it felt like the first of many goodbyes between them. He didn't know why the fact of her leaving hit him broadside. He'd always known that when she recovered her strength and her confidence she would go. He'd wanted that for her. He just hadn't wanted it so soon.

"Matthew, you're so edgy. Please, relax. The press did not follow us. No one did."

Matt rolled his shoulders, glanced in the rearview mirror of the black Lexus he rarely drove, favoring his SUV. As far as he could tell, no one had followed them out of High Stakes. The press didn't know that Helena was with him. If Yungst and Johannes hadn't figured out where she was staying yet, they soon would—and that was what was making him edgy. That and this quick stop before the press conference he had arranged at the club. Helena, in the dark about the danger she might still be in, wanted to see his friend Jamie Morris who she befriended on the plane before she met with the press. Even though he'd wanted to tell her no, he couldn't without revealing that she may be in danger.

So stopping at Jamie's was the first leg of a journey that had acid churning in his stomach. He made himself relax when they pulled up outside her house.

"Would you like to come in with me?" she asked when he rounded his car and opened the door for her.

He shook his head. "You'll want to see her alone. Give her my best. I'll wait out here for you."

Then he settled in to watch and to wait. And to hope that he hadn't made a mistake exposing her to the unknown risks that were out there, lurking.

Helena embraced the younger woman when she opened the door, taken again with Jamie Morris's blond, fresh-faced beauty. "I've been worried about you," she confessed, when they were seated at either end of Jamie's sofa after a chorus of smiling hellos.

"Helena, you don't need to worry about me. You're the one who was hurt. I was so glad when I found out you were out of the hospital, but I've hated it that I didn't know where you were. You've been with Matt this entire time?"

"I'm sorry. I never thought," Helena said. "I should have called. And before you ask, I'm fine. Really fine." It wasn't until she'd said it out loud that Helena realized the truth of her words. She *was* fine. Everything was going to *be* fine. And the sooner she got on with her life, the better.

She wasn't so sure, however, that things were well with Jamie. "The question, Jamie, is how are you doing?"

Jamie shrugged a shoulder. A look came over her face that Helena could only think of as lost before she hid it behind a cheery smile. "I'm okay."

"But not as okay as you would have me think?" she prompted gently. "You've had a bit of a shake up in your life, too."

When Jamie didn't respond, Helena reached out and took her hand. "I know you were looking forward to flying to Asterland and becoming Albert Payune's bride. And I'm sorry for that disappointment. But, Jamie, if you haven't already reconsidered and decided not to follow through with this mail-order marriage, please think about what I've already shared with you. My opinion of Albert Payune has not changed. He was a loyal follower of my late cousin Ivan. Ivan—well, Ivan was not a good man, Jamie. Ivan was power hungry and weak and the source of much grief for my country. I cannot help but think that Albert is very much like Ivan. I don't know what Albert is up to, but I fear that his motives for marrying you are not as pure as he had presented them."

Jamie rose, walked to the window. "Well, you can quit

worrying, Helena. There isn't going to be a wedding. Not now. Evidently not ever. My father...." She ran her fingers along the edge of the curtain, hesitated. "Well, this was my father's grand scheme and since he seems to have disappeared, Albert also seems to have had a change of heart."

"Jamie." Relieved but concerned for Jamie, Helena rose and went to her. She placed a hand on her shoulder. "I'm sorry for the hurt this has caused you. But I'm not sorry that you won't be marrying Albert."

"Let's face it," Jamie said on a long sigh, "I only agreed to the marriage arrangement in hopes that my dad would put the money Albert paid him back into the family farm. And frankly, I wanted to get away from Royal. I guess I wanted a shot at a little adventure, you know? But then again, I suppose it was naive to believe that if I didn't like Albert I could just come back to Royal."

Helena turned Jamie toward her, smiled into her velvet green eyes and knew there was more pain in her story than she would let on. "Trust me on this. Payune is a ruthless user of people. You are better off out of it."

When Jamie looked past her, she squeezed her arm gently. "You are a young and lovely woman. Someday—when the time is right, when the man is right—you will wear that beautiful heirloom wedding dress that you showed me. Someday, you will be the bride of a man who loves you."

Jamie tried for a smile. "I won't be holding out a lot of hope for that. But," she said, rallying with a little laugh, "just in case you're right, I suppose I should take the dress to the cleaners and have it prepared for storage because it doesn't look like I'll be wearing it any time soon."

Helena embraced her, thinking that the two of them had more in common than anyone would imagine. Helena was in love with a man who cared for her deeply but did not love her. Jamie had so much love to give to the man who would discover what a gift her love would be.

"I must go," she said before she became maudlin. "I'll be returning to Asterland soon. But we'll keep in touch, all right?"

"I'd like that."

"Me, too. Good-bye, Jamie."

"Good-bye."

"All set?" Matt asked as they sat in his black car outside the rear entrance to the Texas Cattleman's Club.

"Matthew," she said softly but with a small show of impatience, "I have been set for the past fifteen minutes. Why are we still waiting here in the car?" A frown creased her brows.

Just then Matt's cell phone rang.

"Walker," he said, his expression sober. He listened for a moment, then turned around and looked behind them. "Yeah. I see you now, Dakota. Where's Justin? Never mind. He just pulled up. Aaron is already parked ahead of us.

"Okay. It's show time. As soon as I get out—okay. Okay. I know you know the drill. See you inside."

He pocketed the phone. Smiled at Helena. "Time to go make nice."

While he could see she was perplexed, she didn't ask any questions. He did, however, stop her with a hand on her arm. "Your scarf," he insisted. "We talked about this. You need to put it on."

She rolled her eyes, but she did as he asked. "You're having fun with all this cloak-and-dagger, aren't you?" she asked with an exasperated grin.

He gave her a slashing smile. "More than you'll ever know." And then he was out the door.

When he opened Helena's door, Justin, Dakota and Aaron followed suit and out popped three more women, all dressed in black like Helena, all with scarves over their heads and hiding their faces. Winona was with Justin, Pamela with Aaron. With Dakota was a moonlighting policewoman they'd hired to help play out this little charade. Ben, his hands full looking out for Jamie, wasn't a part of this particular event.

Matt had been right to be cautious. The lot was teeming with reporters who quickly closed in on the quartet of cars. He gave a clipped nod and all four men ushered their ladies through the throng to the club's rear entrance door.

With a little luck, when it was time to leave, the press would have as much trouble figuring out which woman was Helena as they would trying to figure out which vehicle she would be leaving in. And after the four of them led them on a wild and merry chase around Royal, Matt would, he hoped, be able to lose them long enough to get Helena back to the ranch before they figured out who was who.

"Ease off," Dakota snarled, bringing up the rear, as the crush closed in.

"Remind me to keep you on the short list if I ever need an intimidation factor again," Matt said with a grim smile as they trooped into the building.

"Any time," Dakota answered, his eyes watchful on the jostling crowd. "Any time at all."

When they were all inside, where her privacy was protected, Matt pulled Helena off into a corner of the room.

"We can call this off at any time," he said, watching her face carefully. Even before she responded, he saw the confidence he was searching for in her eyes.

She smiled up at him. "I'm fine. And it's past time I faced them."

The press conference was called to a close precisely twenty minutes after it had started. Matt had arranged for Hank Langley, owner of the Texas Cattleman's Club, to ride herd over the proceedings. Hank liked nothing better than a good fight, and he held the line like a right tackle for the Dallas Cowboys.

"I said, it's over." Hank's voice bellowed over the microphone when the press, led by Willis Herkner, clamored for one more question and then one more. "What part of *over* don't you understand, boy?" Hank demanded with a scowl that offered absolutely no room for challenge as he escorted Helena from the dais in the main ballroom.

"You okay, darlin'?" Hank asked, his hand supportive at the small of her back as he ushered her through the door and into a private hallway.

"Actually, yes," Helena said and found herself smiling as Matt met her, his face tight with strain. "I am. I'm fine," she assured him.

"You were wonderful." He took her hands in his. "They were eating out of the palm of your hand."

"It's like riding a horse," she said with a victorious smile. "You never forget how to handle the reins."

"Are you still up for meeting with Yungst and Johannes?" he asked and she would have hugged him for the concern in his voice had they not been surrounded by people.

"I'm up for anything," she said with an assurance that spoke of her rediscovered confidence. "Although I can't imagine what I can tell them about the crash that they don't already know."

* * *

"She knows nothing," Milo Yungst said into his cell phone as he and Garth Johannes followed the black Lexus cutting a zigzag path through Royal.

"I grow weary of hearing those words," an enraged Albert Payune snapped, the anger in his voice booming across the transcontinental connection. "And I grow weary of your inept handling of this entire situation. You must get both Lady Helena Reichard and Jamie Morris alone where they are not surrounded by their protectors. And do not tell me one more time that you cannot find Lady Helena! Find her. These men—these Cattleman's Club men— they are mere businessmen. How can they continue to out- smart you—you who were hand picked to aid the cause?"

"We will find her, sir."

"Yes. You will find her. And you will find out what she knows about the jewels. I'll expect a report in the morning."

The line went dead. Yungst, cold eyes dead ahead, pock- eted the phone. "Follow that car," he ordered Johannes in a thick voice. "We must not fail. We must not."

She would miss this land, Helena thought as she stood on the terrace at High Stakes watching a sunset that was so magnificent it brought tears to her eyes. Bleeding shades of the richest red, the most vibrant fuchsia, the most stun- ning violet, arrested the horizon in shimmering banks of clouds rimmed in gold.

"There is nothing of beauty that compares to this," she whispered as she leaned back against Matthew's chest, rel- ishing his solid strength even as she began missing the shelter of his arms, the electric heat of his loving.

"I disagree." He turned her in his arms. His eyes searched her face, as if memorizing every detail. "If I was a poet, I'd tell you in verse that your beauty rivals any sunset Texas or I have ever seen.''

She smiled into his eyes, her heart breaking for all that she would lose when she left him. ''You are a lovely man, Matthew Walker.''

''And you were incredible today. You were very brave.''

''Well,'' she rested her hands on his shoulders, ''it was time, don't you think? I've been hiding out here long enough.''

''Hiding? No. Try recovering.''

He was being kind when they both knew that hiding out was exactly what she'd been doing.

''I can never thank you for what you've given me. No,'' she interrupted with the press of her finger to his lips when he would have corrected her. ''I need to say this. I have healed here, Matthew. You played no small part in that. You offered me shelter, you offered me sanctuary. You offered me Jewell,'' she said, and felt tears misting her eyes.

''It was a setup from the beginning, wasn't it? You knew I needed her as much as she needed me.''

''It was a risk,'' he said. ''I was worried that I might have done the wrong thing.''

She leaned into him, hugged him hard when his arms banded around her. ''No one has ever risked that much for me.''

The kiss he pressed to the top of her head warmed places in her heart that had been cold for as long as she remembered.

''You looked wonderful on her today.''

''Oh, and it felt wonderful,'' she said, thinking back to the afternoon. Her heart had been in her throat, her palms damp with perspiration as she'd gathered the reins and with assistance from Matthew, mounted the little mare. They'd made two slow but victorious trips around the arena, Jewell favoring her leg but bravely carrying both her weight and Helena's.

"It still feels wonderful," she added, pulling back to touch a hand to his face, "so wonderful to discover that I not only want, but I need to get my life back on course. I have so many projects that have been placed on hold. And so many new ones I want to initiate," she added, thinking of the burn victims who had suffered so much more than she had.

He smiled at her, a bit sadly, she thought, then leaned down to kiss her, long and sweet and slow. "Dance with me," he said, still looking into her eyes.

"I…" she stopped herself, realizing that she'd been about to say, I can't. She smiled instead. "I'd love to."

And there, as the sun set mellow and slow, as the twilight breeze transitioned to a warm caress and the day gave way to the most gentle of nights, she danced, as she'd never thought she would dance again. In the circle of her tall green-eyed Texan's arms, she felt invincible. In the warmth of his embrace she felt loved.

But not enough.

She laid her head against his shoulder. He did love her. She was sure of it. But loving her and wanting to love her were two different things. Matthew did not want to love her. She might never know what held him back, but she would always know the pain his resistance fostered. And if she were to truly get on with her life, she had to leave him. Soon. While she still had the strength to walk away.

Ten

Frank's voice boomed over the intercom, waking Matt at sunrise with a clipped, "Get down here, we've got trouble."

He left Helena sleeping and tore down to the kitchen. He was still zipping and tucking and carrying his boots when he found Frank making coffee.

"What?" he asked flatly.

"We got us a varmint slinking around. The two-legged kind."

Matt dropped his boots and tugged them on. "Where?" he demanded and headed for the door.

"Just cool your jets. He's gone." Frank leaned back against the counter, crossed his arms over his chest and yawned. "Didn't know what woke me, but I figure now it must have been him."

"Him? You got a look at him?"

"Tall. Fence-pole thin. Bushy hair."

"Yungst." Matt swore under his breath.

"You know him?"

"Yeah. I know him. Tell me what happened."

"Well, he was sort of prowling around the barns when I spotted him. Looked to me like he was heading for the big house. That's when I decided to get ol' Bess here locked and loaded." He nodded toward the sixteen-gauge shotgun propped in the corner by the door.

"Well, he got one look at me and lit out like a road-runner with his tail feathers on fire. And no, I didn't get a look at his face or the horsepower he rode out on. Musta had someone waiting behind the wheel, motor revved and ready."

"You're sure he's gone?"

Frank snorted. "Oh yeah. They left a trail of dust as wild as a whirlwind."

Matt settled himself down then met Frank's eye. "I want a man stationed at every door, all three houses. Get Buck and Homer to stand at the front entrance—Les and Gary at South Trail. Anyone comes in, I want to know about it."

Frank squinted at him, his expression grim. "You s'pose it might be time you filled me in on what the heck's goin' on around here?"

"Yes, Matthew."

He spun around to see Helena, sleep-tousled and wrapped in his blue robe, standing uncertainly in the doorway.

"I think it's time you filled us all in."

Helena was steady but still stunned by the time Matt had told the three of them—Lois had joined them over coffee—about the jewel theft, the murder, the suspicions about a planned hostile takeover of Asterland and finally, the Cattleman's Club members' suspicions that Helena and Jamie were in danger. She was so quiet he was worried about her after Frank and Lois left.

"Tell me what you're thinking." He faced her across the table, a mug of cooling coffee clutched between his palms.

"I don't know what to think." She met his eyes, then glanced away. "Missing jewels, a murder." She shook her head. "You…you were watching over me from the beginning?"

He nodded and could see the thoughts racing through her mind.

"And you think…you honestly think there is the possibility of an attempted overthrow of my government?" She shuddered, then met his eyes again, hers startlingly bright as she rose to her feet. "King Bertram. We must warn him. We must—"

"Helena," Matt stopped her with a look. "Please. Sit down."

Reluctantly she sat. He could see her pulse racing at her throat. "We're on top of it. Justin, Aaron, Ben and Dakota. We've been on this since the beginning. I can't have you contacting King Bertram. It might tip our hand. Those who need to know have all been apprised of the situation."

She forced herself to settle. Drew a deep breath. "Payune," she said abruptly. "Albert Payune is behind this. I know it. He and his minions—" Her eyes grew wide, her hand flew to her throat. "Oh, my God. That man. The tall one."

"Yungst," Matthew prompted, all of his senses on red alert.

"Yes. No." She pressed her fingers to her temple. "His name is wrong. I…I can't recall it but it is not Yungst. I know now why he seemed so familiar to me. He's changed his hair, lost some weight, but he was once a royal body-guard. He went underground when it was discovered that he was an anarchist leader. Matthew—we must stop him. He is a wanted man in my country.''

Matt rose, squeezed her hand in reassurance and reached for the phone. He punched in a number and waited, his jaw bunched with impatience.

''Lewis,'' he said when a groggy Dakota picked up on the seventh ring. ''We've got a big bingo here.''

He filled Dakota in on what had happened and the fact that Helena had ID'd Yungst.

''Yeah. Yeah,'' he repeated, agreeing with Dakota's conclusion that they needed to alert the authorities and have both Johannes and Yungst—or whoever he was—picked up. ''Call the others would you, and fill them in? Call Ben first. These guys are getting desperate. He may need to tighten his security on Jamie.''

He hated the look in Helena's eyes as he hung up the phone. He hated even more that he could do very little to alleviate it.

''Jamie. Jamie may be in danger, too?''

''Jamie will be fine,'' he assured her. ''Ben has that situation well in hand.''

He, however, had completely lost control of his situation, he realized as he watched her. The blue eyes that regarded him did so with a growing sense of hurt.

''I could have told you,'' he said, reading her thoughts and preempting the accusation that was sure to come. ''I chose not to.

''You were still recovering, Helena,'' he pointed out when she looked away, pride and betrayal drifting like a shadow across her expressive face. ''You had enough to deal with.''

''Of course,'' she said bitterly, ''weak, insipid soul that

I am, I could not have been expected to survive such dreadful goings-on.''

He frowned. ''That's not what I thought.''

She rose, pinned him with a look where he sat. ''And that is our dilemma then, isn't it, Matthew? I don't know what you think. I don't know what you feel.''

Her anger was swift and surprising. She'd never pressed him about his feelings for her. On some level, he'd wished she would. On another, he'd been relieved that she hadn't. He didn't want to hurt her. But he couldn't give her what he suspected she wanted. He couldn't give her what she deserved.

''And you, you know everything there is to know about me,'' she added, her eyes hurting as she stared at him.

He swallowed, but said nothing.

''Everything but this. I love you.''

He closed his eyes. Slowly shook his head. Let the words roll over him, around him, seep into his blood and burrow deep.

He didn't know what to say. He'd known. He'd known that she had fallen in love with him. Just as he'd known that circumstance had dictated the conditions of that love. She was dependent upon him. She felt indebted to him. But she had a life that she needed to live without him.

''Helena. This…this has all been very hard for you. I care deeply for you. I know you care for me. But you don't love me.''

''Don't.'' Her eyes were hard, her chin high. ''Do not dare to presume to tell me what I feel. You are the one man, Matthew, the one man I have ever loved.''

She swallowed hard and held his gaze. ''I have waited. I have waited a long time. I have waited, and I have wondered how love feels. So don't tell me that I don't love you. I do. I know how it feels.

"I think you know, too," she said after a long moment. "But I think, perhaps, that I am not the only one who has been afraid to face certain truths."

He just stood there, feeling her hurt, knowing, perhaps that what she said was true. Not knowing how he felt about it.

"You will miss me, Matthew Walker," she said sadly before she turned away from him. "You will miss me when I'm gone."

He watched her walk out of the room. And he told himself it didn't carve a crater-size hole in his chest. Told himself it was a righteous decision to let her go. That it was best for her. Best for him.

And yet all he could do right then was stand there, stare at the empty space where she had been—and wonder at another emptiness. The one that left an ache so hollow and so huge, he felt it like an open wound.

Matt wasn't sure what compelled him to follow her a few minutes later. He wasn't even sure what he was going to say, but when he reached her bedroom and saw an open suitcase on her bed, he had to dig deep to find a steady breath.

"You're packing."

He stood in the doorway of her bedroom, watched her stiffen, draw a bracing breath, then toss another item in the suitcase.

"I'll be moving to the Royalton this morning. I've already called for a car to come and pick me up."

With deliberately slow steps, he walked farther into the room, telling himself the panic he felt had to do with her safety, not the cutting fact that she was leaving. Now. This minute.

"Helena. This isn't necessary. It isn't even wise. At

least wait until we're sure the authorities have picked up Yungst and Johannes and begun the extradition process.''

She straightened, finally turned to face him. Her eyes were dry, her soft features set with purpose. ''You've done your duty, Matthew. You've been the perfect host. The perfect protector. The perfect lover.'' Her voice broke slightly before she recovered. ''But it's time for me to go.''

She was serious. She was leaving.

She was leaving. The words bounced around in his head like a battering ram. But the pain, the pain he felt a little lower.

She was leaving, and he knew, without a doubt, that long after she was gone, her memory would cling to him like a shadow. Haunt him like a ghost.

Suddenly, he just couldn't let it go at that. Suddenly he realized that if she left him, he would lose something vital, something more precious than pride, something worth fighting for. Even if the cost was her happiness.

''Don't go.''

She stilled, her slight shoulders stiffening.

''Don't. Go,'' he repeated, his voice sounding rusty.

Very slowly, she turned, searched his face, not at all sure of what she saw there. ''Convince me,'' she said with quiet and regal authority. ''Convince me that I should stay.''

He scrubbed a hand over his face, looked away from those beautiful blue eyes that he knew he would see for the rest of his life, whether she was a part of it or not.

Convince her, she'd said. Hell. What she needed to know wouldn't convince her of anything except the wisdom of leaving. But didn't he owe her at least that much? Didn't he owe her an explanation?

''I was married once,'' he said and waited as if expecting the roof to cave in. She merely stood there. Waiting.

"Jena…Jena had been the queen of the Dallas social strata. She was used to glitz, lived and breathed glamour. And she needed exposure to what she had always referred to as the finer things in life—charity balls, society galas. High Stakes was too far off the beaten path to keep her firmly affixed in the spotlight that her life revolved around.

"We were fresh out of college when I brought her here," he went on, walking to the window and bracing his hand on the sill. "It was probably the biggest mistake I'd ever made."

She was sitting on the bed now, a sweater she'd been packing forgotten in her hand when he turned back to her.

"I thought she would adjust. And at first, it looked like she might. She'd been dazzled by the romantic image of marrying a rancher—then was devastated when the reality of ranch life didn't match the fantasy she'd woven in her mind. She quickly lost her taste for the open range, the dust storms, the solitude."

He shook his head, searching even now, after all these years, for answers that still eluded him. "Even the Cattleman's Club events couldn't make up for the lack of gala functions that were so necessary to her existence."

He cupped a hand to his nape, rolled his shoulders. "I watched a beautiful and vivacious young woman turn into a demanding and insatiable shrew. She hated the ranch. She hated West Texas. And before it was over, she hated me.

"For a long time, I alternated between feeling like I'd failed her and damning her for her inability to adapt. By the time she left me, less than a year into our marriage, I wasn't even sure I still loved her—or if I ever had."

"And now?" she asked softly.

"And now I've pretty much grown to accept that whatever the two of us shared that led us to the altar had been fueled more by hormones and bad judgment than by any true bond.''

Softer still. ''Where is she now?''

He sucked in a breath. Let it out. ''Dead. Six years ago. She was in the Gulf aboard one of our illustrious senator's yachts. There was a party. With Jena, there was always a party,'' he added with more fatigue than bitterness. ''She fell overboard.''

''How…how horrible.''

He met her eyes levelly, feeling little more than a sad apathy for the young life that had been wasted. ''I couldn't make her happy, Helena. I could have tried harder. I could have…I don't know, bent a little. Maybe it wouldn't have ended that way.''

She was quiet for a long time before asking, ''Is that how you see it ending for us, Matthew?''

He met her eyes, begged her to understand. ''I can't change who I am. I couldn't give up High Stakes for her. I can't give it up for you. It's my home. It's in my blood, and to leave it—even for the sake of my marriage—it can never be an option.''

''And you think I would ask you to leave here?''

''I think that, right now, you are as in love with the idea of hiding out here as you are in love with me,'' he said bluntly.

She rose, walked over to him. ''Do you love me, Matthew?''

He touched a hand to her hair. ''I think that I have always loved you,'' he confessed and felt the truth of those words seep into his marrow, settle deep.

Tears rimmed her eyes as she walked into his arms. He drew her close, drowning in the scent of her hair, in the feel of her molded against him.

''Then trust me to know my heart. Trust yourself to

know yours. Above all, trust us to find some common ground together. Believe in us, Matthew." She drew back so she could see his face. "I love you. I love High Stakes. And I stopped hiding days ago. But I'll never stop loving you. Never."

He bent his head to hers, his chest so full of love and want for this woman, he felt the burn behind his eyes. He pinched his eyes shut, gave a brisk shake of his head and knew that whatever he had thought, no matter how noble his intentions, he could never let her go.

"Does this mean I've convinced you?" he asked of her misty blue eyes.

She smiled. "Oh, two little words might seal the deal."

"Marry me," he said without hesitation.

"Yes," she said and brought his mouth down to hers.

Outside the bedroom door, Lois let out a huge sigh of relief. "Well, it's about darn time," she muttered and brushed a tear from her eye as she tottered on down the hall. "Thought that silly little pup was gonna let that woman get away. Take and tan his hide is what I'd do if he hadn't come to his senses.

"Frank!" she bellowed as she trundled down the stairs. "Franklin! We're gonna have us another weddin'! I took and told you so, now didn't I?"

"Yes, ma'am," Frank said as he met her at the bottom of the stairs. "You surely did."

"A countess," she purred, as Frank settled an arm over her shoulders. "Did you ever take and think we'd have us a countess at High Stakes?"

"No, dear. I never did."

They were still in bed when the phone rang the next morning. "Walker," Matt said, tucking Helena under his shoulder and the phone beneath his chin. "Aaron. Hi. What's up?"

"Things are heating up," Aaron said. "I just got a call from Justin. A car attempted to run down Jamie a little while ago."

Matt shot to a sitting position. "My God. I never thought they'd go that far. Is she all right?"

Concerned, Helena raised up on her elbows.

"Yeah. Thank God, Ben was there when it happened and he shoved her out of its path. She took a nasty fall though. When Justin called, he'd just come from the ranch where Ben had taken Jamie. Justin says she'll be fine even though she's shaken and has a knot on her head. According to Justin, Ben really showed his hot Amythra blood. Says he swept her off like in some scene out of the *Arabian Nights*," Aaron added with a grin in his voice.

"I hate that this happened to her, but I'm glad she's out of town and safe with Ben."

Aaron chuckled. "She may be out of danger from this jewel fiasco, but I wouldn't exactly say she's safe. Did you ever notice the look in Ben's eyes whenever her name comes up?"

After a few brief words about how things just kept getting more convoluted, Matt hung up.

Beside him, Helena was practically in tears. "What's going on? What's happened to Jamie?"

"It's okay," he murmured and pulled her close. "Jamie's fine. She's in good hands."

She settled into his embrace, breathed a relieved sigh after he'd filled her in. "And so am I," she said and snuggled in beside him. "I'm in the very best of hands."

Later, after he'd loved her thoroughly and she'd fallen back asleep, he thought back to Aaron's phone call. Ben and Jamie. Could the aloof and mysterious Sheikh Ben

Rassad and sweet, sassy Jamie Morris possibly find what he and Helena had found together?

Doubtful. But then again—he turned and smiled at the Earl of Orion's daughter, naked and warm against his side—stranger things have happened.

* * * * *

Watch for the next installment of the

TEXAS CATTLEMAN'S CLUB:
LONE STAR JEWELS

when oil baron Sheikh Ben Rassad
romances Jamie Morris,
the woman he promised to protect,
and more of the ultra-secret mission
to uncover the missing jewel
is revealed in

HER ARDENT SHEIKH
By Kristi Gold

Coming to you from Silhouette Desire
in April 2001.

And now for a sneak preview of
HER ARDENT SHEIKH,
please turn the page.

One

He had never seen anyone quite so beautiful, nor heard anything quite so intolerable.

Sheikh Ben Rassad pretended to peruse the antiques displayed behind the window as he watched the young woman walk away from the adjacent local dry cleaners.

She clutched a substantial garment covered in clear plastic—and sang in a pitch that could very well wake those who had long since returned to Allah. Ben would not have been surprised if every hound residing in Royal, Texas—pedigreed or of questionable breeding—had joined her in a canine chorus.

She sang with a vengeance, optimism apparent in her voice. She sang of the sun coming out tomorrow, although at the moment bright rays of light burnished her long blond hair blowing in the mild April breeze, turning it to gold. She sang as if tomorrow might not arrive unless she willed it to.

Ben smiled to himself. Her enthusiasm was almost contagious, had she been able to carry a decent tune.

As she strolled the downtown sidewalk, Ben followed a comfortable distance behind his charge while she searched various windows as he had for the past few moments. Although she was small in stature, her faded jeans enhanced her curves, proving that she was, indeed, more woman than girl.

Ben had noticed many pleasing aspects about Jamie Morris in the weeks since he had been assigned to protect her covertly. His fellow Texas Cattleman's Club members had originally requested that he guard her against two persistent men from the small European country of Asterland. The men had been sent to investigate after a plane en route to Asterland had crash-landed just outside Royal—a plane Jamie Morris had been on. She'd been bound for her wedding to Asterland cabinet member Albert Payune, a man with questionable intentions and connections. Jamie had walked away from the crash without serious injury or further obligation to marry. Although the suspected anarchists had returned to their country, she was still not safe. The arranged marriage had come with a price. Quite possibly Jamie's life.

Because of Jamie's ties to Payune, Ben had secretly memorized her habits in order to keep her safe. Guarded her with the same tenacity he utilized in business. Though she was a magnificent creature to behold, duty came first, something he had learned from his upbringing in a country that starkly contrasted with America and its customs.

Now he must protect Jamie from Robert Klimt, a man believed to be Payune's accomplice in planning a revolution in Asterland—someone he suspected to be a murderer and thief. Klimt had escaped not hours before from his hospital bed after languishing for weeks from injuries sustained in a crash. Obviously the club members had under-estimated the man's dangerous determination, and Ben despised the fact that they had not been better prepared.

At the moment, he needed to question Jamie Morris about the crash. Make her aware that he would be her shadow for however long it took to apprehend Klimt. Ensure her safety at all costs. In order to accomplish his goal, she would have to come home with him.

Carefully he planned his approach so as not to frighten her. Yet considering all that she had been through the past few weeks, he doubted she was easily intimidated. And he suspected she would not like what he was about to propose.

But the members of the club depended on him. Little did Jamie Morris know, but so did she.

Jamie took two more steps, stopping at the Royal Confection Shoppe not far from her original location. The song she sang with such passion died on her lips. For that Ben was grateful.

She stared for a long moment at the display of candies with a wistful look of longing. Ben studied her delicate profile, her upturned nose, her full lips, but he'd never quite discerned the color of her eyes. He suspected they were crystalline, like precious stones, reminding him of his family's palace in Amythra, a place far removed from his thoughts more often than not in recent days. Reminding him of Royal's missing legendary red diamond and trusted friend Riley Monroe's murder. Reminding Ben of his mission.

Jamie turned away, but not before Ben caught another glimpse of her plaintive expression. Then she began to whistle as she moved to the curb toward her aged blue sedan parked across the downtown street. He must make his move now.

The squeal of tires heightened Ben's awareness, the bitter taste of danger on his tongue. He glanced toward the grating noise to find that a car was headed in the direction of the sidewalk, aimed at unsuspecting Jamie Morris.

His heart rate accelerated. Sheer instinct and military training thrust him forward, in slow motion it seemed. *Protect her!* screamed out from his brain.

As he reached Jamie, the maniacal car's right front wheel swerved onto the sidewalk. Ben shoved her aside, out of danger, sending her backward onto the concrete in a heap. Her head hit the pavement with a sickening thud. The car sped away.

Ben knelt at her side, his belly knotted with fear—fear that he had caused her more harm in his efforts to save her. "Miss Morris? Are you all right?"

When Jamie attempted to stand, Ben took her arm and helped her to her feet, relieved that she seemed to be without injury.

She grabbed up the bag from where it had landed next to a weathered light pole, carefully brushing one small hand over the plastic surface. "I'm okay."

Concerned over her condition, he grasped her elbow to steady her when she swayed. "Perhaps we should have you examined by a doctor."

She stared at him with a slightly unfocused gaze and as he had suspected, her eyes were light in color, verdant, clear as an oasis pool. A smile tipped the corner of her full lips as she touched the kaffiyeh covering his head. "White sale in progress at Murphy's today?" With that, her eyes drifted shut, and she collapsed into Ben's arms.

He lifted her up, noting how small she felt against him. Fragile. Helpless. Had he failed to protect her after all? If so, he would never forgive himself.

He lowered his ear to her mouth, and her warm breath

fanned his face. He laid his cheek against her left breast and felt the steady beat of her heart. A wave of welcome relief washed over him, and so did an intense need to shelter her.

In March 2001,

Silhouette Desire

presents the next book in

DIANA PALMER's

enthralling *Soldiers of Fortune* trilogy:

THE WINTER SOLDIER

Cy Parks had a reputation around Jacobsville for his taciturn and solitary ways. But spirited Lisa Monroe wasn't put off by the mesmerizing mercenary, and drove him to distraction with her sweetly tantalizing kisses. Though he'd never admit it, Cy was getting mighty possessive of the enchanting woman who needed the type of safeguarding only he could provide. But who would protect the beguiling beauty from *him…?*

Soldiers of Fortune…prisoners of love.

Silhouette®
Where love comes alive™

Available only from Silhouette Desire at your favorite retail outlet.

Visit Silhouette at
www.eHarlequin.com

SDWS

Silhouette®

where love comes alive—online...

eHARLEQUIN.com

your romantic life

●—Romance 101————

♥ Guides to romance, dating and flirting.

●—Dr. Romance ————

♥ Get romance advice and tips from our expert, Dr. Romance.

●—Recipes for Romance —

♥ How to plan romantic meals for you and your sweetie.

●—Daily Love Dose————

♥ Tips on how to keep the romance alive every day.

●—Tales from the Heart——

♥ Discuss romantic dilemmas with other members in our Tales from the Heart message board.

All this and more available at
www.eHarlequin.com
on Women.com Networks

SINTL1R

Get ready to enter the exclusive, masculine world of the...

TEXAS
Cattleman's Club

Silhouette Desire®'s powerful new miniseries features five wealthy Texas bachelors—all members of the state's most prestigious club—who set out on a mission to rescue a princess...and find true love!

TEXAS MILLIONAIRE—August 1999
by Dixie Browning (SD #1232)
CINDERELLA'S TYCOON—September 1999
by Caroline Cross (SD #1238)
BILLIONAIRE BRIDEGROOM—October 1999
by Peggy Moreland (SD #1244)
SECRET AGENT DAD—November 1999
by Metsy Hingle (SD #1250)
LONE STAR PRINCE—December 1999
by Cindy Gerard (SD #1256)

Available at your favorite retail outlet.

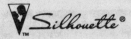

Look us up on-line at: http://www.romance.net   SDTCC

If you enjoyed what you just read,
then we've got an offer you can't resist!

Take 2 bestselling
love stories FREE!

Plus get a FREE surprise gift!

Clip this page and mail it to Silhouette Reader Service™

IN U.S.A.
3010 Walden Ave.
P.O. Box 1867
Buffalo, N.Y. 14240-1867

IN CANADA
P.O. Box 609
Fort Erie, Ontario
L2A 5X3

YES! Please send me 2 free Silhouette Desire® novels and my free surprise gift. Then send me 6 brand-new novels every month, which I will receive months before they're available in stores. In the U.S.A., bill me at the bargain price of $3.34 plus 25¢ delivery per book and applicable sales tax, if any*. In Canada, bill me at the bargain price of $3.74 plus 25¢ delivery per book and applicable taxes**. That's the complete price and a savings of at least 10% off the cover prices—what a great deal! I understand that accepting the 2 free books and gift places me under no obligation ever to buy any books. I can always return a shipment and cancel at any time. Even if I never buy another book from Silhouette, the 2 free books and gift are mine to keep forever. So why not take us up on our invitation. You'll be glad you did!

225 SEN C222
326 SEN C223

Name	(PLEASE PRINT)	
Address	Apt.#	
City	State/Prov.	Zip/Postal Code

* Terms and prices subject to change without notice. Sales tax applicable in N.Y.
** Canadian residents will be charged applicable provincial taxes and GST.
   All orders subject to approval. Offer limited to one per household.
   ® are registered trademarks of Harlequin Enterprises Limited.

DES00   ©1998 Harlequin Enterprises Limited

Desire

January 2001
TALL, DARK & WESTERN
#1339 by Anne Marie Winston

February 2001
THE WAY TO A RANCHER'S HEART
#1345 by Peggy Moreland

March 2001
MILLIONAIRE HUSBAND
#1352 by Leanne Banks
Million-Dollar Men

April 2001
GABRIEL'S GIFT
#1357 by Cait London
Freedom Valley

May 2001
THE TEMPTATION OF
RORY MONAHAN
#1363 by Elizabeth Bevarly

June 2001
A LADY FOR LINCOLN CADE
#1369 by BJ James
Men of Belle Terre

MAN OF THE MONTH

For twenty years Silhouette has been giving
you the ultimate in romantic reads. Come join
the celebration as some of your favorite authors
help celebrate our anniversary with the most
sensual, emotional love stories ever!

Available at your favorite retail outlet.

Silhouette®
Where love comes alive™

Visit Silhouette at www.eHarlequin.com   SDMOM01